C w.

Y0-CBA-769

---

## "Don't move a muscle."

In the blink of an eye, Sam closed the gap between them, clapped one large hand over her mouth and knocked her to the ground with his unyielding body.

He dropped his head beside her ear. His hair tickled her nose. "Listen," he whispered, as he held perfectly still.

At first, Cassie could only hear his breath near her ear and feel his heartbeat and the length of his hard body as she struggled to keep her cool. Then, gradually, she heard sounds she couldn't identify.

"What is it?" she breathed.

"Panther kittens with their mother. We can't disturb them."

"Let me up. Let me see," she whispered frantically.

His eyes warned her to be quiet. "No." He slipped two fingers under her orange crop top. "Too bright."

Cassie gasped at the touch of his rough fingers on her sensitive skin. He didn't move his hand as it rested at the curve of her breast. She looked into his eyes and found them wild, feral and focused on her as his prey.

## ABOUT THE AUTHOR

Jenna McKnight started writing stories when she was
nine, as an antidote to schoolwork. Since retiring from
her work in physical therapy, she's turned to writing
full-time. Jenna makes her home in St. Louis, Missouri,
with her husband and teenage daughter.

## Books by Jenna McKnight

**HARLEQUIN AMERICAN ROMANCE**
426—ELEVEN YEAR MATCH

# Jenna McKnight

## ALLIGATOR ALLEY

# Harlequin Books

TORONTO • NEW YORK • LONDON
AMSTERDAM • PARIS • SYDNEY • HAMBURG
STOCKHOLM • ATHENS • TOKYO • MILAN
MADRID • WARSAW • BUDAPEST • AUCKLAND

To Rich, who shares the adventure.

And to Stacey, who will always share my
memories of large wildcats.

A special thanks to the Saint Louis Zoo, and to
Stephen Bircher, Assistant Curator of Mammals
and Carnivores, for his generous time and
information.

ISBN 0-373-16512-9

ALLIGATOR ALLEY

Copyright © 1993 by V. M. Schweiss.

# Prologue

The vet followed as the wild panther ran for her life, struggling to reach safety in the depths of the Everglades. She leaped over fallen trees, darted through brush, dashed across a glade. He followed with dogs that pulled more men behind them in their eagerness to get the big cat.

She fell, labored to get up, then fell again. She was wounded, exhausted and terrified, and they almost had her. He sensed her desperation to get to a tree, to climb as high as she could in her weakened condition. His heart went out to her.

"There she is!"

"Stay back! Can you get a clear shot?"

"I never got one on the ground before."

"Hurry up. We haven't got all day."

The man raised his rifle, sighting carefully. He had to hit just the right spot.

With one last great attempt, a valiant effort by a desperate animal, the panther struggled to her feet and ducked under a fallen tree. She breathed heavily.

"Hurry up! We haven't got that much time."

The man crept closer to the cornered animal. "Somebody go around to her backside and get her attention. I can't shoot her in the face."

He raised the rifle a second time. "Steady now," he whispered. When the panther turned to snarl at the new threat behind her, presenting a suitable section of her body, the dart flew home. "Got her!"

They didn't have long to wait. The panther was physically depleted from a gunshot wound, under a hundred pounds, in danger of starvation if they didn't get to her first.

As soon as the drug took effect, the men reached under the tree and gently dragged her from her hiding place. "Oh, Lord, look. She's got kittens somewhere."

A nursing female. Shot by poachers, and she had barely escaped with her life. The kittens might already be dead.

"Unless she found a few lame rabbits, she couldn't possibly have eaten enough to keep babies alive."

"There's no telling where they'd be."

"Can't be far. She's got no strength."

"Let's get her stabilized and out of here," the vet said. "If we disturb as little of the swamp as possible, Sam McCord can get in here and find the litter."

"Why not use the dogs?"

"McCord's better. Trust me. He can follow signs even another panther would miss."

# Chapter One

Cassie Osbourne bounced along the old Everglades logging trail in a borrowed Jeep, cursing the man who had lent it to her four hours earlier. Either the thing ran on air, or he hadn't bothered to tell her the gas gauge was stuck on Full. The rudimentary map he'd drawn and handed to her with the words "You can't miss it" was something she was looking forward to balling up and stuffing down his throat—if and when she ever got back to civilization.

Some people called this wilderness a forest, others a swamp, still others the Glades. After driving around in it endlessly for hours, she was inclined to call it the jungle. Thirteen thousand square miles, millions of acres of trees, countless animals, bugs and snakes lay between Lake Okeechobee and Florida Bay. It gave her the willies just to think about it, much less be driving around lost in it.

Logging trails, Indian trails. Whoever had used them first must have had a perverse sense of humor. It looked like one trail as she drove deeper and deeper into the jungle, until she tried to back out. Then she saw the fork.

"I don't believe this," she complained as she banged her fist on the steering wheel. "I've been all over the world and where do I get lost? In Florida! Who the heck gets lost in Florida?"

She was completely and totally surrounded by wall-to-wall vegetation, quite a change for a city girl used to concrete and steel, airplanes, fax machines and the occasional potted plant in public buildings.

Knowing she'd get nowhere by sitting still, she backed into one leg of the fork, shifted into Drive and took the other. Every mile or so, as she was presented with another choice, she began to wonder if she was driving in circles. All she was sure of was that she was lost.

Without warning, the Jeep coasted to a halt beside a mound of dirt and leaves.

"What the—" She stomped on the gas pedal several times. So, it didn't run on air after all. "Terrific," she muttered.

Looking around, she didn't see anything different from what she'd seen all morning. The trees were tall and thick and endless. Everything was still. Instantly she began to feel the heat and humidity, since the breeze she'd created with the moving Jeep was gone.

"Well, Dorothy, welcome to Oz," she whispered as she looked around at the foreign environment. Her grandfather had told her stories about the Everglades, stories of gators and crocs and skeeters and snakes—

"No thanks, I'd rather go home," she replied as she checked for snakes on the ground, stepped out of the Jeep and stretched muscles that had been sitting too long. If answering herself meant she was crazy, then she guessed she was certifiable. "Better do something constructive. Like get out of here alive."

Something constructive. What? Climb to the top of the nearest hill and look for signs of people? The nearest hill was a three-foot mound of dirt that resembled some animal's vacation hideaway. She'd be better off on the hood of the Jeep. Find the nearest stream and follow it downhill? Fat chance of that in the flat Everglades. She opted for the hood.

Minutes later, oblivious to the heat pouring off the dead engine, she felt a chill race up her spine. "Oh, Cassie, what have you gotten yourself into?"

She listened carefully. Noises the Jeep had previously drowned out began to escalate as her presence was accepted for what it was—a lone woman stuck in one spot, with no provisions, no weapon, no way out. Insects buzzed and dive-bombed. Birds chattered and screamed. She heard a bellow that made her heart jump as she realized there was an alligator somewhere nearby.

"You'll be safe as long as you stay in the Jeep," its owner had said. He'd tapped his hollow-sounding leg with a crooked cane. "They don't call this here area Alligator Alley for nothin', you know."

Cassie shivered involuntarily. Alligators on the ground, snakes and spiders in the trees. Where would she be safe?

She climbed back into the Jeep and swatted at a swarm of insects looking for blood. A large bird landed in a nearby tree. It looked like a vulture to her and it, apparently, thought she looked like a good bet for its next meal.

It was time to carefully assess her situation. She had nothing more than a chocolate bar for food. She'd finished the water in her sports bottle an hour ago. The Jeep was an open vehicle with no protection from insects or the elements.

A hissing sound reached her ears. She held absolutely still. It seemed to be coming from under the Jeep, toward the front. After listening to it for a few seconds, she decided she needed a stick—a big one—just in case a snake could slither into the Jeep or drop off an overhanging branch.

She climbed over the back of the seat and edged toward the rear, keeping quiet, moving slowly, listening to the constant hiss. She checked the ground carefully before she turned and slipped one leg out backward.

When she felt something soft and warm on her calf, she froze in midair. She'd checked carefully before; she was afraid to look now. But all those animals her grandfather had mentioned weren't soft or warm. It moved. Its breath was hot. When something rough flicked across her skin, she yanked her leg back in, turned and saw a huge pair of amber eyes in a tawny-colored head. She gasped for breath. The creature put one feline paw up on the back of the Jeep, opened its jaws and showed her some very large, very sharp-looking teeth.

Her eyes darted around the inside of the Jeep, searching for something to throw at the cougar, mountain lion or whatever the hell it was.

It took another swipe at her leg with its tongue.

"At least the vulture would have the decency to wait until I was dead." The cougar appeared capable of doing the job and having its fill first.

Undaunted by her voice, or maybe encouraged by the fear it heard, the cougar crouched ever so slightly, getting ready to spring into the back of the Jeep.

For lack of anything better to do, Cassie screamed bloody murder.

In the blink of an eye, the cat turned and fled, disappearing into the undergrowth so fast she wasn't even sure she'd seen it. The brush closed in on itself once more, not leaving a hint of a path.

"I must be hallucinating." She felt her head to see if she was feverish. Her heart beat faster than it ever had in any race, threatening to burst its way right out of her chest. Her knees shook, and she sat down before she fell down.

Out of the corner of her eye, she saw something move off to her right. Slowly she turned her head that way and scanned the jungle. Carefully she observed every tree trunk, every patch of thick undergrowth. Perhaps the cat was stalking her now. Perhaps there was a pack of them hunting for dinner.

A chill ran up her spine again. If the cats didn't drag her off and eat her, when would her body be found? Months from now? Years? The Jeep would be rusted, her bleached bones slumped in the driver's seat, the key still in the ignition. She'd probably be found by some other poor soul who was just as lost as she. That'd sure make somebody's day.

She wiped the sweat off her face and neck, down to the top of her sports bra. Several dying bugs went with it.

"Hey, lady—"

She vaulted to her feet and turned to find a big, broad, bear of a man standing with one leg up on the Jeep, not three feet from her. Completely taken by surprise, she screamed again, stepped backward, lost her balance and fell off the back of the Jeep.

He walked around to the rear and towered over her. "Yeah, I thought that was you I heard earlier," he said in a voice as rough as his appearance.

She stared up at him from flat on her back. There'd been no warning, no footsteps, no breaking branches. He'd arrived as quietly as the cat. "Tell me I'm not hallucinating."

She knew she wasn't; she couldn't have dreamed up such a rugged specimen. Rough, sturdy, he stood there towering over her as if rooted to the spot, making no move to offer her a hand up. His blond hair was thick, long, wild, set off by the week-old stubble on his face. She wasn't sure she'd want to accept his hand, anyway.

"I take it you saw the panther." His voice was gravelly, almost like a growl, the result, perhaps, of too many years of cigarettes and booze.

So, it had been an elusive Florida panther, not a mountain lion or a cougar. Now that she was faced with this uncivilized looking guy, she wasn't sure which of the two she'd rather deal with. Everything he wore was camouflaged—shorts, T-shirt, backpack—

much as she imagined a poacher would wear to protect himself from the law.

"Which way did he go?"

She rolled to her feet and brushed herself off, ready to run if need be. Never taking wary eyes off him, she pointed over her shoulder.

As quickly as he'd appeared, and without further comment, he headed straight toward where she'd pointed. He carried no rifle, no traps hung from his pack, no pelts dangled from his belt. Maybe he wasn't a poacher.

If there was one person here, it stood to reason there might be more. Maybe she was only half a mile from a house or small town. Maybe she wouldn't die in the Everglades, after all. "Hey, wait a minute," she said.

He looked over his shoulder. "Better get that flat changed if you want to get out of here before dark. You're a long way from the nearest road."

"Flat?" Her eyes located the source of the hissing sound. The front tire was dangerously low. "Well, I'm out of gas, anyway."

She turned back to find him gone, vanished without a sound, as if swallowed up by the jungle. She felt her lifeline give way. If she didn't act fast, her momentary relief at seeing another human being would be just that—momentary. She refused to believe that the pressure she felt behind her eyes and nose had anything to do with the threat of tears. She'd get through this any way she had to, even if it meant trailing along behind a man who moved with no sound, a man who didn't care if she lived or died on the spot.

"Hey! Wait up!" Remembering exactly where the panther had fled into the jungle, she dashed for that same spot. She caught a glimpse of the stranger's backpack and forged ahead, ducking beneath branches and pushing her way through the tangled undergrowth.

He moved quickly, silently, never pausing to wait for her, never acknowledging her presence.

Cassie turned and looked at what she was leaving behind. The view hadn't changed. Tall and dense and green everywhere she looked, with no hint of a path or trail to follow, not a broken branch to indicate which way she'd come. How did he know where he was?

She turned back just in time to see him fading into the jungle again. Fear gripped her anew and her heart felt as though it would beat its way right out of her chest. It was obvious he wasn't lost, and just as obvious that he was leaving her to fend for herself.

Faced with a dilemma, she had to make a quick decision. She could turn and go back to the Jeep, but it was out of gas and had a flat tire. She'd be no closer to finding her way out than before, would just wander around for hours—or days—until something ate her for dinner.

On the other hand, here was a living, breathing man who apparently knew his way around and how to take care of himself in the Everglades. He didn't look starved or dying of thirst. All in all, it seemed a safer bet to follow him than not. He probably had food in his small backpack, and he had a canteen. She had nothing but the clothes on her back.

He walked fast, had almost completely disappeared into the jungle. As a runner in tip-top condition, she had no difficulty catching up to him.

He walked silently. She'd have to keep her eyes on him every second if she didn't want to get left behind.

She was lost and almost alone, but keeping her eyes on his backside was no hardship. Six feet tall, broad at the shoulders, thighs as sturdy as tree trunks and arms to match, he was as light on his feet as a breeze. His dark blond hair carried highlights from the Florida sunshine and was almost long enough in back to gather into a ponytail. Put some tattoos on his arms and he'd make one hell of a longshoreman.

She glanced over her shoulder once more. She'd lost sight of the Jeep. Everywhere she looked, a wall of green looked back, mocking her as a stupid city girl.

"Don't panic," she cautioned herself softly. "Just follow the man."

Stories she'd heard at her grandfather's knee flew back into her mind to taunt and tease her. Snakes and alligators lived in the Everglades, and he'd painted them with vivid words to capture her attention. Snakes hid beneath logs. She jumped over the next rotten log. Alligators submerged themselves in shallow water and waited for their prey, or buried themselves in mud. She vowed to avoid both.

Suddenly the stranger spun around and glared at her with fire in his eyes, causing her to stop on a dime. "Lady, what the hell are you doing?" he demanded, hands on hips. He leaned forward with the most menacing glare she'd ever encountered.

Good question, she thought, feeling very unwelcome and contemplating a step backward. "Following you?"

"Wrong," he declared succinctly. "You're scaring every animal within five miles. I'd like to get a look at that panther before dark. Today." He glared at her, tried to stare her down with wild eyes. There were tiny wrinkles around his blue eyes, evidence of time spent dealing with the harshness of Mother Nature. "Go back to your Jeep, finish your picnic and get the hell out of here."

Soundlessly he turned and hiked off again, faster this time. She followed within ten feet, until she discovered he held tree branches just long enough to let them snap back in her face. "Do you mind?" she asked after the first few smacks.

"Are you still here?"

"I'm lost. Ow! Could you at least not *try* to decapitate me?"

He spun on her again.

"I'm lost," she blurted out. "The Jeep's out of gas. There's no way I can find my way out of here alone."

"You're too noisy. I don't want you around."

"I could be quieter if I wasn't getting smacked in the face by every branch you can find."

"So back off."

"So you can lose me? No thank you."

"Do you have a name?" he demanded.

"Cassie Osbourne." She was surprised when he showed no sign of recognition. She'd won four gold medals in the past two Olympics; he'd have to be a hermit to not know her name.

"Great. Now I know what to write on your grave."
He turned and hiked away.

She was dead if she stayed where she was; she had
no choice but to follow him—a few feet farther back
and as quietly as possible.

When he paused to study some invisible trail, to listen to a hundred different sounds and pick out the one
he wanted to focus on, she paused. She saw nothing
different and couldn't imagine picking one sound out
from the cacophony. When he walked, she walked,
and when he jogged along an old logging trail, she
jogged, always staying twenty feet back.

Five hot, humid, sweaty miles later, he stopped. It
wasn't until he uncapped the canteen and raised it to
his lips that she cautiously narrowed the gap between
them. He drank thirstily, then slowly looked her over
from head to toe. His gaze lingered in spots that made
her nervous, and she felt suddenly conscious of her
skintight spandex shorts and sports bra.

He wiped his forehead on the sleeve of his sweat-
soaked T-shirt. His eyes lingered at the level of her
breasts.

"It sure is humid in here," she commented, hoping
to divert his gaze.

Tempted to wipe the sweat off her face and neck
again, she decided not to do anything to draw attention to her body. She'd raced all over the world wearing no more than what she was wearing now, and in
front of millions of people. Never had she felt so self-
conscious. Never had she been so isolated. If he gave
her trouble, she thought she could outrun him, but

where would that get her? Could a person be more lost than just lost?

She needed to replace all the fluids she'd sweated out in the past ninety minutes. She hoped the water in the canteen was cool, but anything would be better than nothing.

"Always is," he added to her comment on the humidity.

Encouraged that he wasn't yelling at her, she asked, "What's your name?" When he pinned her with a stare meant to discourage her—again—she added, "You know, so I can put it on your grave."

She thought she saw the tiniest hint of amusement sweep through his eyes at her choice of words, but it passed so fast she might have imagined it out of the pure, unadulterated hope that he wasn't some hermit maniac.

"Sam." He capped the canteen, used his sleeve to dry the sweat from his upper lip, then moved on without offering her so much as a swallow.

"Excuse me . . ." Maybe she wasn't any better off following him. Maybe he was just going to keep walking, doing whatever he was out there doing, until she dropped dead behind him, and then he'd just forget he'd ever seen her.

He paused in a small sunlit glade and stared at the ground. "Damn, just what I thought."

Cassie ventured to within ten feet of him, afraid to hear or see what had made him stop. "What is it?" she asked with apprehension, not sure if she wanted to know.

"He's circled around. *He's* been following *us.*"

"Who?"

"The panther."

The hair on the back of her neck stood up, and she whirled around to check behind her. "He's been stalking us?"

"I guess you got the better of his curiosity. You stay here," he ordered.

She grabbed his arm with a speed that surprised even her. He glared down at the small hand wrapped halfway around his sturdy forearm, but her grip didn't lessen, even when he turned that glare directly on her.

"I'm not staying here while you abandon me," she stated with emphasis.

He sighed and ran his other hand over his stubbly jaw. When his eyes paused and lingered on her lips, she released her grasp, though her eyes never left his.

He exhaled a long-suffering sigh. "I'll be back in a little while. A couple of hours at the most."

"A couple of hours?" she shrieked.

"Unless you just scared him halfway to California." His voice approached that growl again. His eyes turned the color of dark steel. "He's not used to shrieking women."

"I'm not staying here alone," she said through gritted teeth. She might die with him, but she knew she'd die without him, and she wasn't ready to sign out yet.

"I'll leave my canteen and backpack with you."

"And leave me for panther bait?"

"Lady, I can leave you with my stuff or I can leave you tied to a tree."

He towered over her, a menacing stance she hoped was all bluff.

She knew when to compromise. "You'll leave the canteen?" she asked.

He slipped out of his backpack and handed her the canteen. "Don't drink it all. It has to last both of us until tomorrow."

"Tomorrow?" She sounded as though he'd said they'd be in the Everglades until next Christmas.

"If I get a look at this panther now, that's how long it'll take me to hike back to my truck."

"Tomorrow?" she squeaked.

"You'll be safe here. Just don't wander away. I'm not going looking for you if you're not here," he warned.

As soon as he melted into the jungle, she helped herself to several deep swallows of the water she'd been craving. She wanted more; she wanted all of it. But she capped the canteen firmly, knowing the water had to last both of them until sometime tomorrow. In her present situation, tomorrow sounded as far away as next year.

It was a relief to be out of the dim interior and back in the sunshine in the glade—for a short while. There was no relief from the humidity there, and after a few minutes, the sun made it worse. Being totally alone in a world she'd never seen before compounded her discomfort.

She edged back toward the cooler shadows of the jungle, keeping Sam's backpack in sight at all times. She also carried the canteen with her, just in case he thought he could sneak back in, get his pack and sneak back out without her. He might not come looking for her, but he'd come looking for his water supply.

There was a rotting, earthy smell about the place. She hoped her lost and dead body wouldn't add to it in the near future.

An hour later, bored with the unchanging surroundings, Cassie searched out a clear spot on the jungle floor, careful to remain within feet of the glade. Kicking sticks and leaves aside, she checked for bugs before she sat down and crossed her legs. This wasn't her favorite position for meditating, but after years of prerace practice, she could do it in any position. She'd have liked to lean back against a tree, but in this godforsaken place, there was no telling what might crawl up or down onto her.

Just before Cassie opened her eyes again, she became aware of a buzzing sound coming from somewhere on the ground in front of her. Slowly she raised her eyelids.

"Oh, Grandpa," she whispered. He'd told her about red-and-black pygmy rattlesnakes. He was right—their rattle did sound like an insect buzz. Frozen to the spot, she tried to remember if he'd told her anything else about them, other than they were poisonous.

This one was coiled between her and the backpack. She couldn't tell how long it was or how far it could strike. It looked small, but this being her first experience with the Everglades and its inhabitants, she opted for discretion. Having no other choice, she decided to wait it out.

Within minutes, the snake had quieted.

Then it began to uncoil slowly.

Tasting vibrations with its tongue, it decided to move out into the glade.

Cassie cautiously rose to her feet to keep an eye on it as it moved away. The canteen slipped from her shoulder and fell to the ground. She froze when the snake turned and looked right at her.

Could snakes hear? This one had no difficulty pinpointing where she was. It turned and slithered toward her. Oh, yeah, now she remembered. Grandpa had said they were aggressive little devils.

She inched backward, one careful step at a time, ever mindful that the glade and the backpack got farther away with each one.

"I'm bigger than you, you stupid snake," she muttered as it advanced on her, driving her farther back into the jungle.

# Chapter Two

"Okay, Grandpa, what would you do now? Yeah, yeah, I know. You'd *survive*." His stories had been full of doing what he'd had to in order to survive. Cassie kept a close watch on the snake as she searched for a stick large enough to protect herself.

She never heard Sam coming, but that didn't surprise her at this point. What did surprise her was when she backed smack-dab into his rock-hard body. It stopped her as effectively as if she'd run into a brick wall. She would have jumped away from him, away from the burning heat of his skin and the slight breath that breezed through her hair, but that would have put her closer to the snake—not a viable option.

"Put the stick down."

His voice rumbled through his chest and into her back, his palpable anger sending shivers up her spine. She pointed at the pygmy rattlesnake, still advancing as though stupid enough to think it had any hope in killing both of them.

"It's poisonous," she whispered.

"It's ten feet away."

"It's following me," she said defensively.

"There're several thousand acres of land around us. I think you can go around."

Was that humor or derision she heard in his voice? She glanced nervously at the undergrowth on either side of them. "There might be more of them in there."

The only thing she heard from Sam was a sigh—a deep, long-suffering sigh that spoke volumes about what a pain she was. Within seconds, before she could react, she felt his steely arm cinch her midsection and lift her off her feet.

"What the— What are you doing?" she shrieked. Even self-defense training hadn't prepared her for such a maneuver.

He stepped around the snake without the slightest bit of hesitation, as though it were nothing more bothersome to him than a gnat.

"Put me down!" she demanded, arms and legs swimming in the air as she desperately tried to find a way to get out of his iron-hard grasp.

"Whatever you say." He dumped her unceremoniously next to his backpack in the glade.

He was laughing at her, she knew it. Even though his lips never cracked a smile, she could see the telltale twinkle in his eyes. She rose to her feet and brushed herself off, seriously considering injuring him. It wouldn't be easy, since he outweighed her by almost a hundred pounds of hard, well-defined muscle.

Sam swung his backpack into place and shouldered the canteen strap. Without further discussion, but with a very annoying, jaunty little whistle, he turned and hiked across the glade.

His actions spoke louder to Cassie than the words he didn't say. Without a doubt, he intended to leave her yet again, to fend for herself, to die in a place where her body would never be found by another human. And to whistle about it? The man was a barbarian.

"You can't lose me that easily," she muttered as she followed him, thanking her lucky stars that she was in such good physical condition.

Grandpa had told her about pygmy rattlesnakes and cottonmouths, coral snakes and alligators, vultures and black-widow spiders. Unfortunately he'd neglected to mention mysterious hermits. She had no idea whether Sam was truly dangerous or a real lifesaver.

As the minutes stretched into hours, she noticed Sam no longer appeared to be tracking. He set a faster pace, what seemed to be a direct line, and seldom stopped to look for panther signs. Not wanting to annoy him further, she followed him without question or comment. She never spoke, never asked for a drink of water and never paused until he stepped into a slough.

"Sam?" Her voice quavered as she called out to him.

He kept on going in water up to his ankles, silent ripples the only indication of his presence in the slough. He never hesitated, never looked over his shoulder to see whether she followed.

She felt her lifeline slipping away again; she just knew he'd picked this route on purpose, since she'd had no trouble following him halfway across the state so far.

The water in the slough was dark, mysterious, hiding its treasures and its monsters beneath a cloak of obscurity. She looked on the surface and along the edge for cottonmouths and alligators but saw nothing reptilian; she knew that was no guarantee of her safety.

"Follow the man," she reminded herself. It still sounded ridiculous, even to her ears. But so did dying alone. She plunged ahead, splashing water as high as her hips as she lunged in and jogged to catch up, her fingers crossed for luck.

Sam paused and waited until she was within twenty feet. "Stay back," he warned.

His clipped words, the steely glare in his eyes, the menacing tone of his voice—any one of those would have been enough to halt her progress. Together they hit her as effectively as a physical blow. She froze. "Why? What is it?" Oh, Lord, if she had to stand there while an alligator swam by, she'd faint.

"Noise attracts gators. Stay away from me."

Spitting mad that all his concern was for himself, she bit the inside of her cheek and managed to hold her temper in check.

She observed him carefully and tried to wade the way he did, noiselessly, making no more sound in the water than the long-legged water birds that stared at them.

She watched the water intently, focusing on every stick, every rock, every turtle, trying to pick out an alligator before it picked her off. Her head pounded with the effort. Her eyes ached. She wiped sweat off her face and sluiced it off her body with her hand, unsure whether it was the result of exertion or fear of what lurked beneath the dark water.

"Cassie . . ." Sam's voice floated back to her.

She glanced up, then gasped. This was it. The big one. The final checkout.

"Stay calm."

"Oh, my God. Is that a cottonmouth?" she squeaked as the long, thin, olive green reptile made its way across the slough. An alligator wouldn't get her today, after all; a snake would.

"'Fraid so."

"Okay, Grandpa," she muttered as she backed away, retracing her steps. "What was I supposed to remember about cottonmouths? Other than they're poisonous, of course."

"Hold still," Sam cautioned.

She stopped dead in water almost up to her knees, praying the snake wouldn't dip beneath the surface and sneak up on her. On that count, she got lucky. On the other hand, it had decided not to cross the slough, after all, but turned and looked at her.

"Sa-am." Fear caused her to draw his name out in two syllables. Is this how it would end? Poisoned in the water, a midnight snack for the alligators? This was no sixteen-inch snake but a full-blown three-footer. Was the insensitive lout just going to stand there and watch?

Because Sam was moving as silently as he always did, and because her eyes were riveted to the reptile, she hadn't known Sam was closing the gap between them until he plucked the snake from the water and flicked it across the slough with one quick snap of his wrist.

She felt . . . traumatized . . . unable to control her reactions. Her knees shook, her heart rate continued to soar past the red zone, the lump in her throat almost choked her, tears burst forth and streamed down her cheeks.

"Oh, damn." Sam dipped his hand in the water for a quick rinse as he stared after the discarded snake.

She was almost too afraid to ask "What?"

He glanced at his hand.

"Did it bite you?" She made those knees work, ran through the water and grabbed his arm, brushed her tears aside and searched his wrist and hand for telltale signs of a bite. Now that she was safe, thanks to him, it would be ironic if he ended up as that midnight snack and she was left to a sure, slow death by starvation.

She saw nothing but tanned skin over steel-cable muscles, covered with a light dusting of blond hair. A diamond eye glistened in the gold panther's-head ring on his pinky.

"No, of course not. I should've saved him for dinner." He stared down at her small hand on his with a look that clearly said she was a bit loony to be examining him for a snake bite.

She dropped his arm like a hot potato. Cottonmouth for dinner? Surely he jested. He didn't want her along, and she recognized it as one more attempt to scare her off. Maybe.

"What is it with you and snakes, anyway?" he demanded.

She had difficulty catching her breath and slowing her heart rate. "You saved my life."

"Don't remind me," he snapped.

"Thank you," she said softly, gratefully, no longer quite so afraid of him. He'd not only saved her, he'd even gone out of his way to do so.

"No big deal." He turned and continued on in the slough the way they'd been going before the snake had appeared.

"It is to me," she said quietly, tired of him turning his back on her every chance he got. She'd find some way to repay him, if it took years. She'd never forget—if she ever actually got out of here alive.

His attitude hadn't changed. He still didn't talk to her, still didn't look back to see if she was following him, either in the slough or back on dry ground. The niggling thought crept into her brain that maybe he'd just saved her out of reflex and was mentally kicking himself for it now. Maybe he really had wanted the snake for dinner.

The next couple of hours of following Sam was hell on Earth. She was hungry. She was thirsty. She was tired. Even in as good a shape as she was, she wanted to stop.

It was with great relief that she saw Sam pause, glance around at the trees at eye level, then set his backpack on a nearby stump. She approached quietly, watched silently as he raised the canteen to his lips, tipped back his head and slurped down some water.

He screwed the cap back on when he was finished. She cleared her throat ever so quietly.

"Are you still here?"

Her stomach growled, drawing his gaze to her bare midsection.

"Here."

It didn't take a genius to hear the anger in his voice or to feel the thrust of it as she caught the canteen he threw at her. She would have thanked him, but thought better of saying anything, given the mood he was in. How could one person be so angry all the time? She didn't think he'd said more than twenty words to her all day, and then they'd been brusque and unfriendly.

All right, so she had rearranged his schedule slightly. Not that he'd volunteered any information in that department, either.

"Do you know how to dig a fire pit?" he asked.

Caught off guard that he'd actually spoken to her first, and expected an answer to boot, she glanced up in surprise. "What?"

"I said, do you know how to dig a fire pit?"

She shrugged. How hard could it be? "Sure. I guess."

He pulled a small spade out of his backpack and pointed to the lucky spot. "Dig down three inches. Stack the dirt carefully around the rim. Tomorrow you're going to put it all back as if we've never been here."

She smiled.

"What's so funny?"

"You just crossed the twenty-word mark."

He frowned and tossed the spade into the ground with enough force to make it stand upright. The glare in his eyes made her think he wished it had been a knife in her body.

"Gather some firewood." He wasn't softening up at all.

She watched him turn and leave again, noting that he'd left both the backpack and the canteen on the stump. He'd be back—unless he was so desperate to get rid of her by now that he was willing to do without all his things.

Digging the fire pit wasn't difficult. Keeping her eyes on the ground for errant snakes and spiders, on the surrounding woods for wild panthers and on the undergrowth for lost alligators while she did the chore was. By the time Sam had returned with a dead animal dangling from his hand, she had enough wood stacked to keep all the monsters away for the night.

"What the—" He stared at the wood. "What the hell are you gonna do with all that?"

She shrugged. "It's firewood."

"It's enough for a week."

She laughed nervously, tempted to mention that she'd expected him to return with a bigger dinner. He must think she was on a diet.

When she caught the fury in his eyes, however, she thought better of it and stifled her laughter. As *generous* as he'd been so far, she wouldn't put it past him to eat it all himself, sit right in front of her and tell her how lip-smacking good it was.

"Put it back."

Her mouth dropped open. "What?" That did it; the man was insane.

"You heard me. Put it back. Don't keep anything thicker than my thumb."

She glanced at his hand. "What is *that?*"

He held it up. "Dinner" was his simple reply. He glanced at the pile of wood again. "I think *I'd* better do the cooking, though. You'd burn the hell out of it."

With great reluctance and dragging feet, she plucked the biggest branches out of the stack of firewood and tossed the first one willy-nilly back into the woods. When that didn't get Sam's ire up, she figured the method was an acceptable one and distributed the rest of the wood in the same way, so that each piece made a lot of noise as it landed.

"Congratulations," he said when she was through.

She smiled.

"Now the entire Everglades knows where we're camped."

Sam busied himself with roasting the animal over a small, hot fire. Cassie cleared a spot across from him, moving leaves and sticks with her foot until she was sure the area was bug-free.

"What is that?" she asked in a much more congenial tone.

"Rabbit."

"Oh." She'd heard rabbit was good. She was hungry enough to eat an armadillo, maybe even a cottonmouth.

Without looking up, she was aware of his eyes on her, leisurely roaming her body, silently appraising her feminine attributes. She pulled her knees up to her chest and wrapped her arms around her shins.

She'd felt safer following him. Then she'd always been behind him, out of his line of sight, twenty feet away. Far enough for a head start if she needed to run away. Now she was within reaching distance, right in front of him, wearing clothes that suddenly felt too skimpy. She could run through any park in America in these clothes, but they didn't seem like enough in the isolated Everglades with an insane hermit sitting just across the tiniest fire she'd ever seen. He could reach right out and—

"It's ready." He broke off a piece of rabbit and held it out to her. His large hand was steady, nonthreatening.

"Thank you," she said as she accepted the hot meat, careful not to let her fingers brush against his.

He watched her as he chewed his food. She stared at the fire. He took his time. She didn't ask for more but was grateful when he offered it.

"You're in pretty good shape."

What did he mean by that? she wondered. Better to change the subject. "I don't understand why you're so mad at me."

He didn't want to answer her, so he didn't. It was as simple as that. He was a man who did what he wanted and enjoyed doing it, and to hell with the rest of the world. If she hadn't figured that out by now, she was too stupid to live.

"You want a list?" he asked after several minutes, in a tone that indicated the question was rhetorical.

She shrugged.

If friends had told him two days ago that he'd be hiking through the swamp with a doll-size, athletic woman trailing behind him, he would have laughed them out of Florida. If they'd described her with thick, strawberry-blond hair, and emerald green eyes that flashed fire at him and burned daggers in his back all day, he'd have told them to dream on. If they'd painted her garb as a bright, skintight running outfit that held no secrets, plastered as it was to her curves, he might have listened a little first.

Although he was sure no one's description of her figure would have painted half as good a picture as he was getting firsthand. He was a man who had been alone a long time, and he thought he must have done some great deed if someone had sent him this package.

He decided to keep his sanity by listing her faults, as he'd offered. It was the least he could do after she'd ruined two full days of tracking the panther. "You're too noisy. You sound like a herd of elephants following me."

She didn't look at him as she slowly chewed the rest of her rabbit.

"You talk to yourself constantly."

She smiled.

She'd heard that one before, and obviously wasn't bothered by it, so he went on. "You're unreliable."

"Now wait just a minute!" Her eyes flashed fire. "No one has ever had reason to say I'm unreliable."

"Did you stay by my backpack in the glade?" No reply. "No, you didn't."

If she wasn't sorry she'd asked, she would be soon. He was still out two days of tracking, three now that he'd spent the entire day with her following him, warning everything away.

"Do go on," she said icily.

"You smell."

She stared at him as though he'd lost his mind. "Excuse me if I didn't put on my hundred-mile deodorant this morning."

He had his hands full remembering he was supposed to be mad at her. It would be very easy to smile at the humor in that cold reply. "That's the problem."

"What?"

"Your deodorant, your shampoo, your toothpaste. The panther can smell all that. He's probably halfway to Texas by now."

"And what brand do you use? Eau d'Everglades?"

"He's used to me."

She finished her rabbit and licked her fingers. "I thought panthers were black."

"Now you know better."

Cassie rested her chin on her knees and gazed at the flickering fire. She looked comfortable enough to get a good night's sleep right there.

He couldn't have that. "And you attract poisonous snakes like nobody's business."

Her eyes grew wide, her back rigid.

"Well, good night," he said as he got effortlessly to his feet. "Don't let the bedbugs bite."

Sam had checked out the trees before selecting this as their campsite. There were two branches just perfect for his string hammock, and he tied it up.

The sun had set; the fire had died out. Little moonlight filtered through the canopy of trees.

"Do snakes climb trees?" she asked.

"All the time."

She sighed. He could barely see her approach his hammock, but he sure enough heard her. She started cleaning house beneath him.

"What the hell are you doing now?" he demanded.

"Clearing a spot to sleep."

The idea was to leave the campsite looking as though a human had never been there. The woman was a menace.

"Beneath me?" Even he wasn't oblivious to the double meaning of that question.

"Well, you said I attract snakes. They're either going to slither up to me, in which case I'm not safe anywhere. Or they're going to fall down out of the tree on top of me, in which case I'm safer under your hammock. They can fall on you."

He grinned. The woman had a death wish for him. Then everything was all right, after all.

"What was that?" she asked five minutes later.

He'd almost been asleep. "What was what?"

"That noise."

He didn't care enough to ask. "Go to sleep."

"There it is again."

He'd been asleep that time. He would have been better off leaving her to the cottonmouth. At least he could get some sleep. "Go to sleep," he ordered.

Minutes later, she jumped up, banging her hard head against his shoulder blade.

"What the—" He vaulted into a sitting position, one leg on each side of the hammock. "What is the matter with you?" he bellowed.

He could hear her rubbing her head where she'd banged into him.

"I felt something slither up against my leg."

He supposed he deserved it for making that crack about snakes right before bedtime. With a loud sigh, meant to give her a guilty conscience—if she was capable of such feelings—he slipped out of the hammock. "All right. If you promise not to make any more noise, you can have the hammock."

"Really?"

The grateful sound in her voice bugged him. Now she'd think he was being nice, when he was only acting in self-defense.

"Thank you." She felt her way around in the dark, brushed against him once and pulled her hand away as though his chest were a hot fire, then slipped into the hammock.

Sam stretched out in the clear spot beneath her. He figured he might as well not waste it, and he would be better off if she *did* attract a snake right out of the tree.

"Sam?"

"Hmm?"

She leaned over to talk to him.

"Don't—"

She fell on to his chest, and almost did him grave bodily harm with her knee.

"—lean over the edge of the hammock," he finished through gritted teeth. "You are the most worthless, useless— Aah!'' he yelled as she scrambled to get off of him.

"Oh! Sam, I'm sorry. Really I am. Sam? Are you all right?"

He groaned. If he could reach her neck . . .

"Sam, speak to me."

She was almost close enough. Just a little closer . . .

"Maybe I'd better just get back in the hammock," she mumbled, barely loud enough for him to hear.

The woman was a menace. If she didn't kill him, she'd kill something else.

No doubt about it, he had to get rid of her.

# Chapter Three

Cassie had spent some long nights lying awake before—nights where she'd mentally run through a race, either before or after the fact. She'd picture herself running, and sometimes it felt as if she were running against a brick wall; she'd never get ahead. She'd hold her breath in silent anticipation of a tough win; eventually she'd gulp in some air and try to remember to breathe normally. The end result was that she'd get herself so tense there was no hope of restful sleep.

This, her first and, she hoped, last night in the jungle, was the same, yet different. She remembered the rattlesnake with great clarity, only it got bigger and faster and more aggressive as the night lengthened. Tossing and turning in Sam's skinny hammock was out of the question, so she lay there with her eyes wide open.

The panther had bigger teeth. The lone vulture multiplied into dozens. Her hissing tire developed into a den of snakes. Vines grabbed at her body, preventing her from following her rescuer out of the jungle.

Each time she managed to fall asleep, she quickly jumped awake as she got lost all over again. Each time she jerked awake, she grabbed the sides of the hammock and held her breath for fear she'd tumble out of it onto the firm body snoring gently beneath her.

It was when she started thinking about his body that she was doomed. She'd done her best to stay away from him all day, to avoid touching him after he'd tumbled her onto the ground in the glade. Then she had to go and actually fall on the man, chest to chest, her face landing on the smooth skin of his neck, one of her hands splayed across massive biceps. He'd seemed even bigger in the dark. And where had her knee landed, of all places?

It seemed as though the night would never end. She kept promising herself they'd reach his truck sometime tomorrow, he'd drop her off somewhere near a bus stop or phone, and she'd spend the next twenty-four hours asleep in her own bed.

SAM YAWNED, stretched, then reached up and smacked Cassie in the rear. "It's morning."

"What?" She started to turn over in the hammock, then caught herself.

"If you fall on top of me again—"

Cassie sat bolt upright, one leg bent over each side of the strings. She frowned as she felt a tingle in the vicinity of her derriere. Had he slapped her bottom to wake her?

Sam eyed the shapely calf dangling right beside him, the expensive running shoe, the exclusive logo on the running sock. None too gently, he swung her leg aside and got up.

Cassie looked around at all the trees and under-growth still surrounding her. Sunlight filtered through the leaves, illuminating the fact that this whole horri-ble experience hadn't been a nightmare, after all—at least not the kind she could wake up from. The fire pit was still there, Sam's backpack still rested on the stump and yes, that was the same old Sam crawling out from beneath the hammock and stretching—ex-cept that he'd spoken to her in a half-human fashion this morning.

She was tempted to lie back and watch the play of his muscles as he stretched and limbered up, but the cold glance he tossed over his shoulder made her re-consider such a foolish and frivolous action. Obvi-ously, morning meant nothing more or less to him than getting her butt out of his hammock and hitting the trail.

"How much longer till we reach your truck?" She gave a token stretch.

Sam's eyes roamed her body from the tip of her fingers, stretched way up over her head, all the way down to her toes. "Just a few hours. You make a lot better time than I would've thought possible."

The gravelly voice that she'd heard for the first time yesterday was somehow comforting today. "I'm sorry," she said quietly.

"What for?"

She shrugged. "Everything. Following you all over creation. Attracting snakes. Ruining whatever it was you were doing out here before you found me." *Kneeing you in the dark,* she added mentally.

He studied her for just a moment, but to Cassie it felt like an eternity. "I was tracking a panther."

She'd gathered that, but waited for him to go on. It seemed that whenever she'd opened her mouth yesterday, she'd made him mad.

"I raised him from a kitten...turned him loose two weeks ago."

That definitely caught her interest. "You raised him?"

He nodded. "They're endangered, you know."

She didn't know.

"I wanted to check on him and be sure he was getting enough food on his own."

"I guess that's instinct, huh?" She continued when he looked at her expectantly, "I mean, stalking and killing food . . . it's instinct, right?"

"Mostly. It helps when the mother shows the kittens what to do with a kill, though."

She pulled out her ponytail holder and ran her fingers through her pale-strawberry-blond waves. She looked at his hair. It didn't look any different than yesterday, which only meant asking him for a comb was a ridiculous thought. He probably didn't even own one.

His eyes darkened as he stared at her body, and she became aware of the picture she presented with her arms up over her head, her breasts thrust forward, her midsection further exposed.

"So, do you do that often?" she asked as she tried to look inconspicuous, quickly bent over and redid her ponytail.

Sam busied himself taking down the hammock and stuffing it into his backpack. "I'd say I've had a hand in about half the panthers left, one way or another."

Cassie looked around at the jungle surrounding them. "I guess I wasn't in as much danger as I thought yesterday when your friend licked my leg."

For the first time, a smile slashed its way across Sam's rugged features, softening his whole appearance, yet not diminishing his masculinity in any way. He paused in his packing, and his gaze immediately fell to the extremity in question.

Cassie was sorry she'd drawn attention—again—to her body. It seemed that no matter what she said or did, the fact remained that she was terribly underdressed for the occasion.

"He *licked* your leg?" he queried. "Is *that* what all that screaming was about?"

She nodded, almost jumping out of her skin when he actually laughed. She was sure she had shock written all over her face that he actually had the capacity for laughter.

"Well, don't look so surprised," he ordered as he read her mind.

Cassie thought she actually saw a twinkle in his navy eyes.

He continued, "I might get the impression you thought I was an ogre or something."

The only rational explanation that entered her mind was that he was a morning person, and she'd just caught him at a bad time yesterday. "Something like that," she muttered. "I didn't know he wasn't wild."

His expression grew serious. "Oh, he's wild all right. Don't let the fact that I raised him fool you. Any one of the panthers out here is entirely capable of bringing you or me down and having a good dinner."

"But you raised him," she objected.

"Makes no difference. A big cat reaches a certain age, and everything changes. Now panthers, they're kind of shy. They'd rather avoid people...normally," he said with a frown.

"What?"

"It kind of bothers me that he approached you. That's not typical behavior. Of course, the way you screamed and scared him off, he might think twice before trying that again."

"Let's hope."

"Cover up the fire pit while I get breakfast."

"Cover it?"

"Yeah. Put the dirt back." He motioned with his hands while he talked. "Make like we've never been here."

"Make like we've never been here?" she muttered as he turned and walked into the jungle, pulling his disappearing act again. "I wish."

Covering the fire pit took all of five minutes. She sat and wondered what was on the menu that they didn't have to cook, and she didn't have long to wait.

Sam returned, carrying his shirt.

Cassie hoped her gasp didn't travel to his ears, but if the man heard as well as he did everything else, she wasn't likely to get off that easily. She tore her eyes away from his broad, muscular chest, though it wasn't easy. While he wasn't muscle-bound, she thought he could go out for pro football tomorrow and put the rest of any team to shame.

He crouched in front of her. "Breakfast," he said quietly as he laid the shirt on the ground between them and opened it.

Cassie stared at the greenery. It looked as if he'd defoliated a couple of bushes. "Excuse me?"

"Think of it as a salad."

She didn't have to look up to see him smiling, she could hear it in his voice.

"I'll tell you, Sam, as a runner I'm pretty much into eating healthy."

"Yeah?" he asked when she paused.

"This ain't it." She risked raising her eyes to look at his face, making sure she didn't linger on his chest.

He looked at the food as though he didn't know what she was talking about. "Well, it might not be what you'd find in the grocery store—"

"It might not even be anything I could identify in an encyclopedia."

He picked up a leaf and chewed on it. "It's all edible. Guaranteed."

Still she didn't help herself.

He spread his arms wide. "Do I appear to be wasting away from lack of food? Look at me."

Cassie prided herself on self-control. But not staring at his tanned, broad chest was the hardest thing she'd done in a long, long time. She scowled at him, then the breakfast. "What's that?"

"What?"

"Something moved."

He glanced around at the trees. "Where?"

"In the salad." She pointed.

Sam reached down, poked a few leaves aside and picked up a green insect. "This?"

She nodded.

"Protein." He opened his mouth.

"No!" She covered her eyes with both hands. She would *not* watch him eat a bug, no matter how insane he was. If this is what being a hermit reduced a person to, then it was overrated.

"Mmm, good," he murmured. He waited until she looked, then tossed the intact, squirming insect over his shoulder. "You should loosen up, lady. Come on. Grab a bite. We'll eat while we walk."

Cassie sighed, resisted the urge to kick him in the shin, then grabbed a handful of green leaves and carefully screened them for anything with legs. Sam gathered up the ends of his shirt and carried the food with him, tossed her the canteen and slipped into his backpack.

"So, you're a runner," he said as they started out on the trail only he could see.

"Yeah." She kept her eyes glued to his backpack, not those wide, wide shoulders. It was difficult, except for the one moment he paused and pointed out a drag mark made by an alligator's tail. Cassie memorized that mark for future reference.

"What do you do for a living?"

She could like this new side of Sam just fine, as long as he didn't pull any more pretend-to-eat-the-bug stunts.

"I run."

He glanced over his shoulder. "For a living?"

She smiled. He really hadn't recognized her name yesterday. "How long have you lived in the boonies?"

"Not long enough that running has become a job description."

The leaves really didn't taste too bad, though the texture was weird. She felt as if any minute now her mother would reach out, slap her hand and tell her not to eat things unless she knew what they were. "I manage to support myself."

"You can't do that forever."

"Tell me about it." She was more than aware that endorsements didn't last forever. "I've already started to make plans. My grandfather left some land to the town he lived in, and they've given it to me to build a factory on."

"You think the world needs more factories?"

She didn't care for his change of tone and didn't want to risk his mood changing, either. She could agree that the world needed better, cheaper running shoes, but she needed a congenial guide out of this jungle in order to accomplish that. Self-preservation foremost in her mind, she changed the subject. "Hey, Sam, what kind of snake is that?"

He dropped the shirt and threw his hands up in the air. "I don't believe this!" he barked as he turned and retraced his steps. "Where?"

She pointed into the undergrowth, surprised that she could remain so calm in the vicinity of a snake after the past two encounters she'd had. She must be getting conditioned to them, though getting used to snakes wouldn't have been something she would have chosen to work on. "In there."

He frowned at her and bent to inspect the foliage. "How could you see a snake in there?"

"Well, it wasn't in there a second ago. It took one look at me and slithered off."

"That's a first," he mumbled. "I can't see anything. What color was it?"

Cassie shrugged, unsure. "It had rings." She was quick to note that he stood up immediately, stiff and very wary.

"What color?"

"Um...red, yellow, and black, I think. Is that bad?"

"It's not good," he growled. He retrieved his shirt and tucked it in his belt—giving it a slight shake first.

Cassie sighed and fell in step behind him. Surely she didn't attract snakes the way he had said. She and Sam were, after all, hiking through some of the densest, most overgrown wilderness in the world. There were bound to be a lot of snakes around.

A branch whipped back into her face. "Sorry about that, Cassie," she muttered sarcastically for him as she dropped back to her customary twenty feet.

"You're talking to yourself again," Sam said with annoyance.

"So what else is new?" It was a habit she'd developed during her training runs, to keep from getting bored. Some people even said she talked to herself during races, but she thought they made that up.

"Oh, no. Not again," she said when Sam stepped into another slough two hours later.

He bent over, reached down and splashed water up onto his face and chest.

Cassie stepped up to the edge and looked around for snakes and alligators. "Is it clean enough for that?" she asked, skeptical and hopeful at the same time.

Sam looked up at her, said nothing and continued with his rinsing.

Cassie slid the canteen to the ground, eased into the water and did the same.

"Don't drink it."

She thought he shared that information rather grudgingly, but since he'd made an attempt to be civil once more, she responded likewise. "I'm sorry for whatever I did to make you mad again."

Sam's sigh was a long one, and he ended it by plunging his head into the water, drenching his long hair.

Cassie bent over to do the same, anticipating the cool wetness as much as any woman who'd been camping and wanted a shower.

"You might not want to do that," he warned.

She paused in mid-bend and looked over at him. "Why's that?"

"Leeches."

Cassie shrieked and sprinted back to the bank, grateful for the warning—for a split second. From her position up on the bank, she could look down on him—not by much, but every inch counted. "So why are you standing in there?" she demanded.

"I get a leech on me, I pull it off. You get one on you, *you* pull it off."

She shuddered at the thought of touching something so disgusting. For him, it was probably no worse than one more annoying insect. "No, you'd have to do it for me."

"I wouldn't *have* to do any such thing," he told her as he glared up at her. "You could deal with it yourself. You seem to be pretty damn independent."

"And that bothers you?"

"Hell no, it doesn't bother me," he roared. "I'm ever-loving *grateful* you're so damn independent that you just drive a Jeep off into the Glades... alone...without food...water...clothes—" he ticked off the list on his fingers "—matches..." His eyes raked her skimpy, skintight clothing. "Obviously without anything other than what God gave you."

"Well, this is no day at the beach for me, either."

Sam squeezed the excess water out of his hair, looking more frustrated than Cassie had seen him look so far. She would have suspected he was so angry because he couldn't stand to see a person get herself caught up in so many predicaments in such a short time, but then he'd have to care first, wouldn't he?

On the other side of the slough, Sam slipped back into his shirt, looking exactly as he had the day before—rough, wild and, most of all, eager to be rid of her. As soon as he resumed his trek toward the truck, Cassie retrieved the canteen and dashed across the narrow slough as quickly as possible, reluctant to get left too far behind.

"Just bite your tongue," she told herself. "You'll be out of here soon, on your way back to your gloriously civilized apartment. You'll never have to see him again." The good news didn't even make her smile, and she could only attribute that to the fact that when he did smile and tease, he was a whole different, likable person.

Sam's pace picked up. Cassie wasn't sure whether that was because he was more determined than ever to lose her—which would be rather silly at this late date—or just eager to get the ordeal over.

A short time later, Sam slowed, paused, listened carefully. Cassie kept her distance until she saw the grim look on his face.

"What's wrong?" she asked as she narrowed the gap between them.

He silenced her with one hand up in the air, halting her progress ten feet from where he stood.

Cassie listened, strained to hear what he heard. It was no use. "Sam—"

In the blink of an eye, Sam closed the space between them, clapped one large hand over her lips and knocked her to the ground with his unyielding body.

There was no way she could lie still for this. But a little voice in the back of her mind reminded her that Sam had saved her life more than once in the past twenty-four hours, and probably wasn't trying to kill her now. She wasn't ready to go for his eyes and blind him for no good reason, but she was still plenty capable of inflicting a lot of pain—or a little warning shot.

Sam groaned as she shifted her knee, a prophesy of more to come if he didn't explain the situation to her satisfaction—fast. He dropped his head beside her ear.

"Listen," he said in a strained voice as he held perfectly still.

Cassie listened. Again she heard nothing. Unless... "What is that?" she asked very quietly, catching his cautious mood. Certainly not a panther; he'd never be afraid of a panther. What else was that big, dangerous enough to have Sam on the ground on top of her, and loose in the Everglades?

Sam raised his head and peered toward the intruder, moving his head this way and that, trying to see through the undergrowth without being seen.

Cassie didn't mind being saved from some vile jungle creature; she did mind a couple of hundred pounds of male bulk pinning her to the ground, moving against her every time he raised, lowered or shifted his head. "Sam—"

His fingertips brushed across her lips, cut off her protest, hovered there steadily.

She whispered ever so softly, "You can get off of me now."

He shook his head, his eyes warning her to keep silent.

"Why not?"

He slipped two fingers beneath the strap of her sports bra. "Too bright."

Cassie almost screamed at the touch of his rough fingers on her sensitive skin. His gesture was entirely impersonal; her response was completely reflexive. So, she was doomed to lie on the hard, uneven ground, beneath his camouflage-clad body, and hide her bright running clothes. For how long? She shifted as well as she was able to with his weight bearing down on her, trying to find a more comfortable position and to ignore the fact that one of his thighs pressed intimately between her legs.

Sam glanced down at her spandex shorts. Dissatisfied with a mere scrap of color showing itself, he splayed his hand across the skin on her thigh, lifted his leg slightly and shoved hers beneath his.

Cassie thought he was carrying this camouflage thing just a little too far, but the increased tension she felt in his body held her in check. Sam was the most self-possessed man she'd ever met. A poisonous snake meant no more to him than an annoying gnat. He tracked full-grown panthers as a matter of course and carried no gun for protection—and she'd seen the teeth on the only big cat she ever hoped to run across this side of a cage. He could find his way through the jungle without a map, compass, food or shelter. If Sam was tense, she'd best just hold still, keep quiet and wait. She could argue about his methods later.

At first, she could only hear him breathing near her ear, feel his heartbeat through her chest, smell his scent as she struggled to keep her cool in this situation. Then, gradually, she could hear what he heard.

Voices, low and quiet. Bodies brushing through the foliage. Boots trampling the undergrowth.

She strained to arch her neck, turn her head and look to the side and behind her, ignoring the fact that the movement put her face and Sam's in proximity and now his rough whiskers brushed the hollow of her cheek. Still she couldn't see anything.

It was difficult to determine anything, even as the hushed voices grew nearer. They quieted as one voice snapped at the others in an undertone.

Cassie held her breath. These were men Sam didn't want to meet up with. A hermit's reaction—or something more? She suspected the latter. She waited for them to pass.

Sam rested his head on his hand. His body weight evened out, enabling Cassie to breathe easier, though she was almost too afraid to breathe at all.

Her lips were poised next to his ear. "Who are they?" she whispered as thin as a breeze.

"Poachers."

She waited for them to move on, but the sounds didn't recede. They changed. She heard metallic sounds, scuffling, canteen lids unscrewing—that she recognized instantly. They were taking a break not twenty feet away.

She craned her neck to see them again. When she saw a camouflaged shoulder lean against a nearby tree, she was sorry she'd looked. Sam must have felt the shock run through her body, because he spread his hand across her face and hugged her close, cocooning her beneath him, hiding her from those men.

Laughter drifted over to Sam and her, then was cut off with a muffled curse. She smelled cigarette smoke as it wafted over the rotting, earthy smell of the ground on which they lay. She hoped the jungle was too moist for a stray butt to accidentally start a fire.

Aeons later, the sounds changed again. She saw more movement as the men rose to their feet. She saw more than she wanted as one man visited a nearby tree, his back to her, a hunting rifle slung across his torso. At that point, she closed her eyes, held her breath and hoped he rejoined his comrades without looking around first.

Time stretched on, to eternity and beyond. Cassie hadn't been this scared when she'd thought she was going to die in the Jeep. That was frightened; this was earth-shattering, knee-shaking, heart-stopping petrified. Against half a dozen men weighted down with weapons, she and Sam had no choice other than to hide.

The sounds of the group receded. Cassie could hear the zipper drag its way home before the man rushed off to join the others.

She turned to look again, to check and see if they were in the clear. Sam raised his head and turned to whisper in her ear at the same time, only it wasn't her ear that was closest to him. His lips brushed hers, sending sparks of a whole different voltage shooting through her body. Accident or not, time stood still as his wild navy eyes locked with her emerald green ones.

He caught his lower lip between his teeth, as though to erase a tickle—or to stop the kind of electricity she felt. The intimacy of their bodies drew Cassie's thoughts to things she'd rather not think about—not now, not with Sam, not ever.

"Is it safe to move?" she whispered in a raspy voice, reluctant to clear her throat for fear it would make too much noise, attract the poachers back to the area and keep Sam on top of her.

He grinned down at her. "What do you think?"

She placed both hands against the broad wall of his chest and pushed, but to no avail. "I think it's time for you to get off me." The man didn't budge; she might as well have been trapped under a full-grown oak. "Before—"

His grin still firmly in place, he responded, "Before what?"

He made no move to ease away from her. His mouth still hovered just inches above hers, his heartbeat still echoed through her chest.

His devilish grin now only served to remind her how fast his good mood had disappeared earlier that same morning. "Before I manage to get my knee loose again," she said, finishing her threat.

"Really?" His head dipped lower, and as he let his cheek brush over her hair and softly move a tendril, he moved his thigh back to its former resting place between her legs, pressing it against her ever so slightly.

She smothered a feminine gasp that came unbidden from deep within. "I also bite."

His head snapped up. "And here I was just thinking of taking a siesta."

"I'm sure you were." She wiggled free, sat up and brushed off leaves, twigs and various creepy insects.

Sam rose to his knees, gazed around for stragglers, then stood up and towered over her. He held out his hand.

Cassie glanced up, saw the proffered hand and looked up to his face. This man, who'd tried his darnedest to get rid of her, was offering assistance? Her small hand in his was a satisfying sight, but she quickly moved onto neutral ground. "Who were those guys?"

He sighed. "Leroy Watson and his two boys. I didn't recognize the others."

"Just how dangerous are they?"

He grinned devilishly. "Depends on how mad they are about someone raiding their cabin while they were gone. I heard that several expensive rifles were damaged beyond repair."

Cassie returned his grin. "You heard that, did you? I guess that could make them even more dangerous?"

"Well, right now, if I had my choice between running into them or wrestling a gator with one arm tied behind my back, I'd take the gator. I'd be sure to die either way, but the gator would be a lot quicker."

Cassie shuddered at the picture he'd drawn. And yesterday, she'd thought all she had to worry about were reptiles and spiders.

Again Cassie was allowed to walk directly behind Sam, beside him when they traversed a wider logging trail, rather than dodging branches or falling back to the relatively safer distance of twenty feet. This time she listened as they traveled, wondering how Sam could have possibly heard the poachers minutes before she had. She heard chattering birds, buzzing insects, an occasional splash in the distance.

Sam, too, seemed rather occupied with listening, more so than usual. Of course, she was usually quite far behind him, so she wasn't sure if that was true or if she was just more tuned in to their surroundings now that she'd found out there were things inherently more dangerous, more mysterious, more intent on remaining undetected than wild animals.

An hour later, she almost fell over his pickup truck. If it had been a snake, she'd be dead.

"We're here!" she exclaimed in delight when she practically ran into the camouflaged hood. "My gosh, if we'd been twenty feet to either side, I never would've seen it."

Sam grinned down at her. "That's the general idea." He shrugged out of his pack, tossed it into the open truck bed without looking, then turned back to her, rubbing his hands in anticipation. "I've got some supplies behind the seat. How about we break open a can of peaches?"

Cassie slipped the canteen off her shoulder. It took a second to realize they weren't alone.

"The idea of canned food's got you speechless, huh?" Sam teased.

It took another second for Cassie to catch her breath. She raised her hand to point, opened her mouth to yell a warning, watched in fear as the tawny head rose higher and higher out of the bed of the truck, directly behind Sam.

There were no more seconds left. Paws came up, landed soundlessly on the side, leaped into the air. Its mouth opened, teeth flashed, a hundred pounds of fur, bone and muscle flew toward Sam's back.

Sam was quick on his feet, but not quick enough. He only had time to duck slightly, throwing himself off balance enough that the panther's added weight on his neck dragged them both down.

"Sam!" Cassie screamed.

His forehead hit the closest tree with a cracking sound. His legs buckled beneath him. The panther wrapped itself around Sam's torso, gnawed on his neck and shoulder, looked as possessive as any wild animal that had just brought down a deer for its next meal.

# Chapter Four

Frightened beyond all rational thought, Cassie reached down to the ground, grabbed anything she could find and threw it at the cat. Leaves, twigs and dirt flew fast and furious. When she found a dead branch big enough to do some damage, she wielded it like a club and charged.

She rushed in close, screaming like a banshee, dodging around this way and that, hoping the panther would think there were three of her threatening one of it. Sam lay as still as death, face down on the ground next to the tree with the panther on top of him.

The panther released its hold on Sam's neck to snarl at Cassie. It still had its forelegs wrapped around his torso in a wild-animal body hug.

Cassie reached out with the four-foot stick and poked the cat in its muscular shoulder.

It batted at the branch, caught it with its front claws and nearly ripped it out of her grasp.

Cassie screamed. It had worked back by her Jeep. Sam had said the panther wasn't used to shrieking women. That was fair; she wasn't used to panthers. She only hoped it was the same one.

As the panther paused to stare at her, Cassie took hold of the stick like a baseball bat and swung. Hard.

The impact wasn't what she expected. It was muffled, as any hit on a fur-covered body would be, but it sent shock waves up her arms as though she'd just made contact with a solid tree trunk. This was not an animal she wanted jumping on her.

Cassie was quickly debating on her next brilliant move, when the panther turned tail and dodged into the undergrowth. Shocked at its quick departure when she was expecting a retaliatory attack, Cassie dropped the stick and stared after the disappearing animal.

"Sam!" She fell to her knees beside his body. She didn't know where to begin. "Oh, my God."

She touched his rock-solid arm with her left hand, his broad back with her right. He was littered with the twigs and leaves and debris she'd thrown at his attacker—not a great way to treat gaping, bloody wounds.

"Sam?" she said in confusion.

He had no gaping or bloody wounds. In fact, as her fingers brushed over his inert body, she noticed there was no blood anywhere.

With her fingertips she examined his T-shirt. It was wet over the shoulder and upper back where he'd been tasted by the panther. *Kissed* was more like it, she realized.

A groan emanated from deep within his throat. As he began to stir, Cassie lent a helping hand to roll him over onto his back. "Oh, my God. Don't move, Sam. I'll find something."

She took one last look at the blood on his forehead as she rose to retrieve the canteen and search for some cloth. "The man finally finds his panther and what does he do? He hits his head on a tree and passes out."

"Oh, God, you're doing it again," Sam said with a groan that accentuated the gravel in his deep voice.

"Sam?" Cassie sunk to her knees by his side. "Can you talk to me?"

"Why should I? You talk to yourself just fine."

"Open your eyes, Sam." She poured water on a T-shirt she'd grabbed from his backpack and dabbed the cloth on his forehead.

"Ow!" His eyes flew open, and he shoved one hand out in resistance as he scooted away. His hand landed on her chest, cupping one breast as he held her at bay.

Cassie was glad to see he was capable of feeling pain.

Sam's hand fell away as he collapsed onto his back. "What the hell...? Where...?" He swallowed, opened his eyes again and stared at Cassie, then slumped onto his back. "Oh, God, I thought you were a nightmare."

Cassie's smile was all too sugary sweet as she reached out and dabbed at his head wound again.

"Hey!" His iron grip on her wrist deterred her. "The tree was bad enough, thank you very much."

"I'm just trying to help," she said innocently. "That needs cleaning."

Sam touched his forehead, then examined the blood on his fingers with a frown.

"What's the matter? Never seen your own blood before?"

He stared at his red fingers for a few seconds, then perused the area, his truck, finally letting his eyes linger on Cassie. "Oh, yeah. I remember. Go ahead, clean away."

Cassie was just about to toss the wet cloth at him and tell him to do his own damn first aid, when he closed his eyes and relaxed. "Oh, what the hell?" she mumbled.

She leaned over him.

"You can pour water over it to flush it."

She glanced down to see him staring at her sports bra. She felt like pouring water on him, all right.

"There's more in the truck. We'll be fine."

Cassie dabbed harder, but he never groaned again. He didn't even wince as she pulled splinters of bark out of his skin.

"You're sure there's more water?" she asked, still leaning over him as she paused.

"I'm sure."

"You're not hallucinating or dreaming or something? We're out here in the Everglades...miles from...wherever...." Her voice trailed off. He could have been killed.

"I'm sure," he growled.

"You'd better be." She washed the wound with the contents of the canteen, then checked one more time.

"Are you about done poking around?" he queried.

Cassie sat back on her heels. "Just checking."

"What for, for chrissakes?"

She shot to her feet, tossing the wet T-shirt onto his chest and throwing the canteen down onto his flat belly. "I was just making sure it was clean so you wouldn't get an infection."

"Making sure I won't die on you is more like it."

She felt like kicking dirt in his face.

"Oh, for chrissakes, you're not going to cry, are you? I'm the one injured here."

*Never,* Cassie thought. *Not in front of an ogre like you.* She bit her tongue to be sure.

Sam rose to one knee, then to both feet. He swayed and grabbed the nearest tree with one hand.

"Sam!" All bitterness aside, Cassie slid herself under his other arm. With her free hand, she grabbed his stubbled chin and turned his head.

He tried to bat her away, but his aim wasn't good.

Cassie stared into his navy eyes. Her knowledge of first aid was basically limited to running injuries and heat exhaustion. His eyes, while having lost some of their clarity and focus, exhibited no uneven pupil changes. "I think you better sit back down, Sam." She bent her knees to encourage him to lower himself. He weighed heavily on her shoulder.

"No, I'll be all right." He tried to step away from the tree, his large body depending on her smaller one.

"Sure you will, big guy." Cassie patted him on his broad chest. She bent her knees even more, but still he wouldn't sit down and rest. "Easy does it now."

"The truck."

"The truck's fine."

"No." He pushed himself away from the tree, taking her with him. "I want to get to the truck."

Cassie grinned. "What's the matter, Sam? Are you afraid to sit on the ground with all the bugs and snakes?"

His snort clued her in to the fact that he was at least coherent. "In your dreams, lady. I want my peaches."

"Sam leaned heavily against the truck while he directed Cassie to the location of several cans of fruit, a can opener, utensils and additional water.

"All the comforts of home," he said with a grin.

Cassie didn't particularly want to see his home if the inside of his truck behind the seat was representative.

"Did you see him?" Sam asked as he speared a peach in the can with his fork.

Cassie looked up from her applesauce; it tasted like nectar of the gods after two days in the jungle living off rabbit and green leaves.

"I mean," Sam corrected, "did you *see* him."

She frowned. "Maybe you're not supposed to be eating solid food right after a head injury."

"My head's fine."

"Then why are your eyes moving around like that?"

"Like what?"

"Kind of glazed and wandering."

"What do you expect?" he bellowed. "You go crack a tree with your head and let's see how your eyes look."

Cassie snickered.

"What?"

"You probably did crack it. Your head's hard enough."

"Enough about me. Did you *see*—"

"Yes, I saw him," she snapped. "I was throwing things and charging him with a stick in my hand to protect *you*."

Sam brushed some dirt off his well-defined biceps. "I wondered how I got so dirty. How did he look?"

She took her own sweet time answering, not to make him suffer, but to relive the scene. A shiver ran up her spine. "Big. Fast. Strong."

"Skinny?"

"No way," she answered quickly. "That cat looked healthy."

She marveled at how both man and beast looked similar—blond or golden, wild, enough muscles to propel them safely through the jungle. And something more elemental—lack of fear. The panther had the good sense to turn tail and run, but it hadn't seemed frightened. She didn't think Sam would ever show fear, even if cornered by half a dozen poachers. Caution, yes. But fear? The word seemed incongruous in relation to Sam.

"Like he had enough to eat?"

"He left you in one piece, didn't he?"

Sam speared another peach. He couldn't count on Cassie's untrained eye to give him the information he had to have. "Well, maybe he didn't go too far."

"Yeah, well, it won't matter now." Cassie finished her can of fruit and stood up. "Let's get going."

Sam leaned back against the front tire of the truck. "Go? We can't leave yet." He gazed up at her, worried about the damage done to his head as he realized the body beneath those skintight running clothes was looking mighty tasty. Too bad. When he gave her the rest of his news, she was going to be madder than he'd seen her yet. That much he knew without a doubt.

Cassie tapped her toe in the dirt, waiting.

Sam struggled to his feet, not wanting to be sitting on the ground at the mercy of her fury when she exploded. "I've got to see that panther for myself."

Fury didn't describe the expression in her emerald eyes. Volcanic, maybe. Piercing, definitely.

Murderous, without a doubt.

"Look, we've got food and water," he added in a moment of weakness. Damn his throbbing head. "We'll stay here tonight. I'll search for him in the morning." He felt as though he were trying to talk a hurricane out of striking.

"And if you don't find him in the morning?" she asked icily.

"Then I search for him in the afternoon."

"And then—"

The flash of emerald fire didn't sway him.

"We stay until we run out of food and water, if need be," he decreed.

"Fine," she snapped.

He stared at her warily, making a mental note to be sure his knife was safely in his pocket before he fell asleep. "Fine?"

"Yes, fine." She'd seen his supplies. If she ate her fill, they wouldn't last past breakfast. "Where's the can opener? I'm starving."

"I'VE GOT DIBS on the cab," Cassie stated as Sam rooted through his backpack. The sun was setting, and not a moment too soon. She was exhausted.

Sam glanced up at the sky and remarked, "It's getting dark kind of early tonight."

"Yeah, well, I'm not hunting for firewood. I'm going to bed." To emphasize that she meant what she said, she stood up and walked to the cab of the truck. "Have you got a flashlight?"

Without a word, Sam crossed the few feet between them. Cassie held her ground. This cab was hers tonight, and she wouldn't be intimidated out of it. One sleepless night in his hammock was enough to last her forever.

Her back to the open doorway, her rear against the seat, Cassie leaned backward as Sam towered over her. His navy eyes locked with hers as he reached around her and opened the glove compartment.

As his chest brushed against her breasts, she leaned even farther backward, in danger of reclining right back on the bench seat. Another second of this, and she'd be spending another sleepless night, after all.

"Your flashlight," he said as he held it out to her.

It took her several minutes to regain her composure after he flashed her a wicked grin, turned and resumed rooting through his backpack.

She mumbled as she shone the light into the cab. "God's gift to women . . . egotistical jerk . . ."

"What? Can't hear you."

"Yeah, lucky for you," she continued quietly, knowing all he could probably hear was the buzz of her voice and hoping she was driving him nuts. "What I'm thinking about you would singe your ears. . . ."

His quiet chuckle drove her on, and she continued her muttering as she played the light around inside the truck. Nothing crawling on the ceiling. Dash was fine. The vinyl bench seat was cracked and peeling, so that its insides were exposed; it was probably providing a haven for some enterprising insect hiding from her beam. No snakes on the bare metal floor. She gritted her teeth and checked under the seat, dreading what she might find nesting there. Nothing, thank God.

With a sigh of relief, she flicked off the flashlight and returned it to the glove compartment, closed the door, stretched out on the seat as well as she was able to and plunked the door lock down with her heel.

Sam's laugh penetrated the tightly closed cab.

*PIT. PAT. PIT. PAT.*

Cassie had always loved the sound of rain on the roof. It made for a good night's sleep no matter what country she was in, no matter what her accommodations. Besides the relaxing sound, a good rain cleared the air and lowered the heat and humidity for racing.

She curled up on her side and went back to sleep with a relaxed smile on her face, hands folded beneath her cheek.

She ignored the sound of someone trying to work the door handle.

"Cassie."

She ignored the tapping on the window.

"Cassie, open up."

The banging on the window was a bit harder to sleep through.

"What?" she snapped, still curled up on her side. If he and his gravelly voice would just go away right now, she'd be able to go back to her dream.

"Open up. It's raining out here." Sam patted his pockets, trying in vain to find the key.

She sighed as she reached for the lock. He *had* saved her life. Memories of how he'd lain on top of her to hide her from the poachers sent her scooting all the way over to the far side as Sam seemed to fill the cab with his large body.

Memories of how he'd teased her with his leg afterward had her plastering herself against the driver's-side door.

"Damn," Sam muttered as he picked at the camouflaged T-shirt stuck to his chest. "I'm soaked." He stripped it over his head in one smooth motion, right there in front of her, and tossed it up on the dashboard.

Cassie cleared her throat and struggled to suggest "Maybe you should get out and get your gear." *A dry shirt would be nice.* "Before it gets wet."

"It's under the truck. I figured there wouldn't be any extra room in here with the two of us."

*No kidding.* For a man who seemed as large as all outdoors when she'd met him in the middle of nowhere, not in the least diminished in size by the trees towering around him, there was just too much male presence about him to be contained in the cab of a truck. Especially the truck she was in.

She could barely breathe.

Cassie didn't have to look outside to see that she couldn't send him back out there. The tempo of the rain on the roof had picked up considerably since she'd been sleeping a very comfortable sleep, under the circumstances. But looking through the windshield at the almost-black night was a heck of a lot safer and saner than staring at his naked chest just three feet from her. If she was lucky, it would quit raining soon and he could go back to his hammock.

Yet she hadn't been very lucky lately.

Sam fell asleep almost immediately, slightly reclined in the angle made by the door and the seat back. His legs stretched past the gearshift lever, nearly reaching the pedals on her side. Rather than vie with him for leg room on the floor, Cassie pulled her feet up on the bench seat between them.

With Sam asleep, his breathing deep and rhythmical, she was free to stare wherever her eyes roamed. Who'd ever know? When would she ever get to study such a specimen of masculinity again?

Never, she was sure. There was little hair on Sam's chest, but what was there tapered off and pointed downward—down over his hard, flat belly, down until it dipped into the waistband of his shorts and disappeared from her view.

He was wearing shorts that exposed those tree-trunk-sturdy thighs, dusted with just enough hair to make Cassie wonder if they felt as rough as he appeared.

If she wanted, if she moved her foot just a few inches, she could reach out with a bare toe and find out for herself. He was asleep. He'd never know.

As if on cue, Sam stirred, squirmed to get a little more comfortable. He never opened his eyes.

Cassie studied his profile, the strong chin and jaw. She remembered his perfect white teeth from one of the few smiles he'd graced her with. His stubble had grown heavier, darker blond than his sun-streaked hair, a lock had fallen toward the cut on his forehead, pointing at it as a reminder of all she had endured in less than forty-eight hours.

Exhausting hours, she remembered as she drifted off.

*ENOUGH*! SAM THOUGHT. He'd had enough of her kicking in the past hour. He'd always thought of himself as a patient man, especially around panthers and children, but an hour of getting kicked in the thigh every time he dropped off to sleep for a few minutes was asking too much.

He clamped a hand around her slim ankle and knew, the second he felt her smooth skin beneath his calluses, he shouldn't have touched her.

He studied her there, plastered up against the far door, one hand under her cheek, several strands of pale strawberry-blond hair pulled free from her ponytail to curl delicately around her temple and drape across her cheekbone. The stubborn jaw was relaxed, her lips slightly parted.

His gaze lingered longer than it should have—if he intended to sleep peacefully—then drifted lower. He liked it better when sports bras were worn *under* other clothes. Not that he minded looking at a woman running through the streets in one, of course, but being stuck in a truck cab all night with a woman wearing one... Its lemon-yellow color caught even the faintest glimmer and magnified it a hundred times. It drew his eyes like a beacon to her breasts, full mounds smashed beneath the shiny fabric, too full to be flattened as the bra intended.

His gaze traveled downward, over the flat stomach, over the skintight, geometric-print spandex shorts that had threatened to blind him when he'd first seen her standing in her Jeep, scouting the Glades for who knew what.

Her leg twitched again, trying to kick out. Her long, smooth, shapely leg. Muscles strong enough to enable her to keep up with him for two days in no way took away from their femininity.

She kicked harder, trying to throw off his grasp, though she was still asleep.

Sam lay his head back on the seat for a moment and closed his eyes. It was either that or he'd find himself memorizing her body. There was no hope for him in this situation.

As soon as she kicked him again, he slid his hand higher up, gliding over her smooth skin, higher still.

A big mistake.

"What—" Cassie's eyes flew open as one masculine hand gripped her thigh above the knee, while the other held her upper arm. Without a second's hesitation, without any thought, she landed one foot in Sam's ribs—hard—the other in his thigh muscle.

"Damn," he cursed as he released her instantly, then added, "What the hell's the matter with you?"

She stared at him.

He noted no fear, only a wary look to see what he was going to do next. If she had any sense, he thought she should be afraid. He was a lot bigger than she was.

"You've been kicking me all night," he stated.

"Then keep your injured body on your side of the truck."

"You kick me there, too."

"Don't grab me."

"Listen, you've been kicking me for the past hour. You twitch in your sleep like a dog dreaming after a rabbit. I'd rather you sleep over here so you kick the door instead of me."

"Over there? You're leaving?"

They both listened to the slow, continuous rain.

"No, I'm not leaving. Come over here, use me for a pillow so I can get some sleep. My thigh's going to be black-and-blue in the morning."

He watched as she lowered her eyes and stared at his bare chest. So, she wasn't as indifferent as she pretended. He also knew that if she saw him grin at that knowledge, she'd kick him again.

"Come on." He slowly, tentatively reached for her arm, lightly grasped her slender wrist, methodically circled it with his fingers and gently tugged it toward him. "You can lean against me. I'm bound to be more comfortable than that hard door."

She resisted slightly.

"Just to sleep. Come on. You can lean on me or put your head in my lap." He felt himself harden at the thought of her head anywhere near his lap, and his mouth went dry. "I don't care. Just don't kick me anymore, all right?"

Apparently the thought of her head in his lap also didn't seem safe to her, because she chose to lean against him. She felt good tucked beneath his arm, her head on his shoulder, her back pressed to his rib cage.

What to do with his arm? He couldn't leave it up along the back of the seat all night. He couldn't drape it over her shoulder and across her breasts. Surely he'd find himself out in the rain in the blink of an eye if he tried that.

He slid it down close to the seat back and let his hand rest next to her hip as she faced sideways and stretched her legs out along the seat.

"What's wrong?" she asked as he fidgeted.

He poked at her ponytail. "Whatever's in your hair is scratchy. Do you mind?" He didn't wait to find out, but gave her elastic ponytail holder a gentle tug and dragged it out of her hair.

Another mistake. Now her soft, coconut-scented waves tickled his chest.

"Good night," he said with a smile, knowing he wouldn't sleep, suddenly not caring.

"Sam?"

"Hmm?"

"Do you think you'll be able to find your panther in the morning?"

He nodded against the top of her head, reached up with his free hand and smoothed down some of the tickly ends. He let his fingers catch and linger in the waves left by the ponytail band. "Probably. He knows the truck. Depends on how bad you scared him."

Silence.

He hadn't meant to sound critical. "What *did* you do to him, anyway?"

"You mean before I screamed?"

"Mmm-hmm. Besides throwing whatever you could find."

"You don't want to know."

Sam thought about it. "You probably kicked him," he guessed.

He was surprised when a light, feminine chuckle reached his ears, even more surprised when he felt his arm tighten momentarily around her torso in response.

"I didn't get that close. But I didn't damage him if that's what you're worried about. He'll be fine for whatever you raised him for."

"If you get me started talking about panthers, we'll be awake all night," he warned.

She shrugged. "So, it's late. Make it a bedtime story. Capsulize it for me."

"Capsulize? How can I condense the fact that there are only about thirty Florida panthers still alive?"

Cassie heard the passion and pain in his voice.

"I've got a few on my ranch for breeding, and I release one when I can, trying to get their numbers up. I can go on for hours about how I select them, check their DNA to ensure genetic variation.... I've spent fifteen years doing this. I can't capsulize it."

"You just did," she said softly.

"But I didn't tell you—"

He sounded frustrated, as though there was so much more to say.

"All right. Never mind. You try it."

"What?"

"Capsulize the past fifteen years of your life before we nod off here."

She yawned, covering her mouth.

He shook her by jiggling his shoulder. "Come on. Fair's fair."

Again he heard that chuckle, as warm and welcome as wind chimes tinkling in the breeze. He jiggled his shoulder again to get her going. Her head bounced lightly against him; her hair brushed over his skin. It no longer tickled; it screamed at him for attention.

"Fifteen years in fifteen seconds, hmm?" She thought for a moment.

Sam was just about to jiggle her again, in case she'd fallen asleep. No reason he should suffer alone.

"Running."

"You told me that earlier."

"Hush. It's my turn. I ran track in the past two Olympics, won four gold medals—"

"Really?" he interrupted, lifting his head to peer down at her. "You're not pulling my leg?"

"No."

"You really won gold medals?"

"Yes."

"Distance, obviously, since you've had no trouble keeping up with me."

Her hair tickled his chest again as she nodded and laughed at him taking her story time. "Yes. Now do I get to finish or are you taking over?"

"Go ahead."

"I've been raising financial backing so I can build a running-shoe factory near my parents' hometown. I've got a lot of family there who supported me while I ran. And with the bad economy, most of them are out of work now."

"Sounds like a big project for one person."

"My secretary keeps me organized. She—"

"Time's up. See what I mean? It's impossible—"

"You're impossible."

Sam grinned and rested his head on top of hers as she wiggled into a more comfortable position. "Yeah, I know."

His eyes closed, but sleep wasn't on his mind. With the slightest tilt of his head, his lips brushed against the top of her head, buried themselves in her soft hair. His arm might be pinned between her and the seat back, but his hand was free to inch its way across the smooth skin of her ribs. His other hand slid lightly up her arm, then down again. Comfortingly. Soothingly.

Hopefully.

"Sam." Cassie rotated her head to look up at him.

Her tone wasn't demanding, he noted, nor was it threatening. It was more of a question. He answered by feathering kisses on top of her head, working his way downward, toward her ear, then her temple.

Cassie's hand moved—involuntarily—and landed on Sam's taut thigh. She felt his reaction all through his body as every muscle jerked and tensed, then his hands zeroed in on her.

They were on her upper arms, her body, turning her around to face him, pulling her knees up until they rested on his thighs. His lips never stopped touching her, kissing her lightly everywhere—her hair, her face, her neck—until she thought she would scream at the overpowering deliciousness of it all. When she didn't refuse, didn't scream or slap him, he grew bolder, yet remained oh so gentle. The contrast between his strength and tenderness was overwhelming, possessing, undeniable.

A sigh escaped her lips as she felt herself drawn toward him, ever closer. She felt his breath on her face, his racing heart beneath her hand, his hardness under her knee. She tried to tell herself this was crazy, but she wasn't listening. She didn't want to listen. He was big and strong and safe, and, heaven forbid, she found herself wanting him.

Just as that realization clobbered her, an ear-splitting crash jerked her right out of Sam's grasp.

"What?" he whispered.

"What the hell was that?" she asked, her body shaking from excitement, from fear, from indecision.

He reached for her, slid one hand behind her hips and scooted her tense body toward him again. "It was nothing. Just a tree falling."

She braced herself stiffly over his chest, and he knew without a doubt that he wanted to go ax that damned tree into tiny splinters and burn it for fuel.

"This is crazy," she declared breathlessly. "What if the poachers find us here?"

"On a night like this?" The skeptical look he shot her said he knew she wasn't really worried about poachers. He watched as she struggled within herself, as mood drifted away and changed.

"Maybe I'd better..." She motioned toward the driver's side of the truck but couldn't form the words. She gestured helplessly.

"And start kicking me again? No way."

"Sam."

He could see her indecision on her face, hear it in her uncertain voice. Nobody said he had to like it. With determination and resolve, he spun her around on the seat until she was cradled beneath his arm again, back where she'd started. Any resistance on her part was no match for his strength. Not that she resisted too hard. "Okay?" he asked.

Her breath escaped in a small sigh. Apparently she was satisfied with his actions. At least one of them was.

DAWN DROVE Sam out of the truck cab. Waking up with Cassie curled into his side, in his arms, both knees resting in his lap—that was asking too much of him in the light of day. At night, her hair had smelled like fresh coconut. She'd been soft, yet firm, where they'd touched. She'd been a lot easier to resist in the dark when she hadn't been practically in his lap, one small hand resting quietly on his fly.

He got out of there, leaving his door open, before she woke up. He made a hundred-foot circle around the area to see what he could find in the way of panther signs.

As he approached the rear of the truck, he wished he had a camera.

Cassie shot out the driver's side with a high-pitched squeal and slammed the door behind her. The panther Sam had been searching for flew out the other. It hit the ground running, smart cat that it was, and breezed right past him.

"Did you see that?" Cassie screamed at Sam, pale strawberry-blond waves cascading every which way around her face and over her shoulders.

He grinned. "Wouldn't have missed it for the world. You put the fear of God into that cat."

"I—" she sputtered. "That thing could've eaten me for breakfast." She rubbed her palm over one side of her neck. "I think it licked me again."

Sam just stood there.

"Well, aren't you going to follow it before it gets away?"

"What for?"

Her eyes narrowed until he couldn't see the green in them anymore. He tried to contain himself with the good news.

"What do you mean, 'what for?' What are you out here for?" she demanded, fists on her hips, fury in her stance.

"To see him. Now I've seen him. He looks fine."

Her eyes widened. "You mean ... we can go?"

As the good news dawned on her, she broke into a smile and dashed into the passenger side of the truck.

Sam laughed to see her so relieved. "Yes, we can go. But don't break a leg in your hurry."

"Not a chance. Come on. Come on."

"I guess you don't want breakfast first," he teased as he got behind the wheel.

"I want breakfast, all right. Pancakes and scrambled eggs. I can't wait to get home. Drive." She bounced around on the seat, as giddy as a child.

"Well, I don't know how long that'll be. I don't know where you live. But I do know where I'm going. *My* home."

"Your home?" The bouncing ended. "Why would I want to go to your home?"

"Get a grip, lady. It's my truck. We're going to my ranch."

Cassie sank back against the seat. "Oh, hell. Just drive. Anything's better than this."

# Chapter Five

The ancient truck joggled along the logging trails, over and through the ruts, for the better part of two hours. Cassie braced herself as best she could to keep from ricocheting off the cracked seat, but it wasn't easy.

"Why don't you have seat belts in this thing?" she snapped after she'd had to brace herself against the dashboard for the umpteenth time.

"Too old."

She couldn't wait to leave the jungle behind, get out on the highway and breeze off to wherever he lived.

It never happened.

They did manage to get out onto a gravel road, where the truck kicked up a terrific amount of dust in its wake, but they were only on it a short time before Sam turned into a long, half-hidden drive.

"What's this?" she asked unnecessarily as he parked the truck, afraid she already knew the answer.

"My ranch."

That was exactly what she'd been afraid of. They hadn't even left the jungle, not really. They'd just changed locations. She still felt as far from home as ever.

If Cassie hadn't been lost in the Everglades for two days, she might have appreciated Sam's secluded ranch as much as she loved her grandfather's tiny refuge from the big city.

Tucked beneath a canopy of sheltering trees, Sam's small house blended with its environment with simplistic beauty. The wide, wooden porch opened its arms in welcome. The dark house fused into the trees and promised cloistered comfort.

But she had been in the jungle for two long, seemingly endless days, and she didn't appreciate this new location one whit.

"Don't look so down. You can have the first shower."

Her eyebrows rose. He thought *that* would cheer her up? He thought *that* could replace her apartment? Her apartment with her own phone, her own shower, her clean clothes? He had a lot to learn about women.

He grinned. "Don't tell me you thought I didn't have a shower."

She looked at the small house and shrugged. Who knew how little a hermit needed to keep him happy? "This far out in the middle of nowhere...."

"I even have a phone and electricity."

"Okay," she said with a sigh. "I'll start with the shower, then use the phone." She might as well get clean. This ranch was probably hours from her apartment. She couldn't stand to be dirty much longer.

Cassie glanced around as she climbed the three porch steps. A hundred yards off to her left, across a small clearing, were high chain-link pens. She could see several panthers within, and an older man hosing down the concrete. Sam tossed him a wave before he led Cassie across the porch and held the screen door for her.

Who would have thought the man had manners? After the way he'd treated her in the jungle, she would have bet he didn't hold doors open for women. Funny how returning to civilization had changed him—if you could call this civilization.

Sam led the way into the house. There was no entry or foyer, just the main room. From the looks of it, it appeared to be the room he spent most of his time in, and shared with a few wild animals, as well. Both arms of the threadbare sofa were chewed into stubs, so that the foam-rubber stuffing was exposed. One side of it and the banged-up coffee table were littered with newspapers, held down by three coffee mugs and an empty doughnut box. The latter was in the process of being shredded by a large, red parrot.

"George!" Sam boomed.

If a parrot could look guilty, that one did as it ducked its head and fluttered to the floor. Its nails clicked across the tile as it scuttered away from the scene of the crime.

"Out!" Sam held the door open until the long tail was completely in the clear.

"Won't he fly away?"

"I have problems keeping him out, not keeping him in. The day he chews my computer is the day he goes back to starring in a bird show in Kissimmee."

Sam quickly crossed the bare floor to the far corner and carefully checked his computer—a real up-to-date one from the looks of it—for damage. "All he does is scream, every morning and every night."

Cassie's eyes were drawn upward, over the computer, to a whole wallful of the most beautiful photographs she had ever seen. "Sam, these are wonderful."

"Oh." He barely glanced up as he checked the cables. "Thanks."

"You took them?" There were captured images of playful kittens, loving mothers, lusting males, hunting predators. But in black-and-white, with nothing to distract from the reality, they spoke volumes of Sam's love and admiration for his endangered panthers.

"Yeah. Over the years."

The man became more confusing by the minute, his hermit-maniac image tarnished forever. If she'd thought he had no feelings, proof to the contrary was plastered all over the wall.

"Shower's this way." He led her through the kitchen.

Cassie shuddered. He might have feelings, but he didn't have an inkling where to begin housekeeping if the dirty dishes in the sink were any indication. Or else he'd left monkeys in charge while he was gone. Cabinet doors stood open, drawers weren't closed, towels trailed everywhere.

The bedroom was next. Cassie wasn't surprised to find the bed unmade, the sheet rumpled, dirty clothes in the corner. She tried not to look. She wouldn't be here long.

Sam reached down and picked up a pair of black briefs. "Sorry about the mess," he mumbled, then tossed the briefs into the closet. "I spend most of my time outside."

There was only one door left. She was almost afraid to look.

"There's a linen closet in the bathroom. Help yourself to whatever you need."

He stepped out of her way and watched while she went in and closed the door.

Cassie leaned back against it and sighed. Used washcloths were draped stiffly over the edge of the sink and the top of the shower doors, having dried out during Sam's absence. She tried to console herself with the fact that at least he kept himself clean, if nothing else.

Surprisingly, Cassie found everything she needed except conditioner. Disposable razors, shampoo, soap, a fresh washcloth and towel, hot water—she was in blissful heaven as clean water cascaded over her body for ten minutes before she heard the door open.

"Cassie? It's Sam."

"No kidding," she muttered, wishing for more steam to coat the glass shower door and hide her from his view. She hovered back in the farthest corner, using her hands and washcloth to hide anything that might be visible, wondering just what he *could* see. And that kind of thinking quickly turned into wishing the tables were turned and musing about what she'd be able to see of him in his shower.

"I brought you a T-shirt and some shorts."

"Oh." Her snappy complaint regarding his intrusion died before she'd had a chance to voice it. Clean clothes? "Thanks, Sam."

"Anything else I can get you?"

If he only knew. "Uh, no. Thanks."

"Save me some hot water."

She stared into space after he left, wondering why she hadn't bitten his head off. He could have left the clothes outside the door. He could have waited until she was out of the shower and covered by a towel.

"He could have let you put your dirty clothes back on, too," she scolded herself, shutting off the water before she used up all the hot. "Or he could have invited himself in." She flushed hotly, and knew it wasn't from the steam.

Sam leaned back against the outside of the bathroom door and closed his eyes. If he'd only known . . . he'd never have gone in there. He lived alone; he didn't even close the bathroom door when he showered. It never occurred to him that the shower doors were see-through. Steamy, but not steamy enough.

When he heard the water stop, he stepped away from the door, not wanting her to think he was waiting to pounce on her. He wasn't even aware that he'd started cleaning the kitchen until he found himself scrubbing the table.

He stopped immediately. There was no need to alter his life-style because he had a guest for a couple of hours—a guest who had made it clear last night that she'd had a moment of weakness in the darkness and didn't want to follow up on it. It was his turn for a shower, and maybe it would have to be a cold one, after all.

He entered the bedroom from the kitchen, she from the bathroom.

As expected, the T-shirt was all too huge and hung over her thighs. When Cassie tugged one side of the large neck up to cover her right shoulder, it slipped off the other, and was in danger of exposing the uppermost portion of her well-rounded breast. The light-gray T-shirt had darker spots where her wet hair had touched and dripped.

Sam swallowed—definitely a cold shower. Thank God he hadn't given her a white shirt.

"I guess..." He cleared his throat. "I guess the shorts were too big, too?"

She giggled.

No, not a giggle, he thought. A light, sweet laugh, slightly embarrassed, totally feminine and delightful.

"Good thing they have a drawstring," she acknowledged. "What did you do with my clothes?"

"I threw them in the washer. As soon as I'm done in the shower, I'll turn them on."

Three little words. *Turn them on.* They had nothing to do with Cassie and him—not then and there, anyway—but staring at her luscious body, naked inside his T-shirt, made those three little words ring in his ears as he remembered her passionate response the night before—in the dark. If he had to describe how she looked right now, in the light of day, he'd have to say friendly, maybe vulnerable. *Receptive* was questionable.

If he stood there drooling over her any longer, she'd think he was an animal. "If you go outside, be sure to stay in the clearing," he said as he abruptly closed the bathroom door.

Cassie was used to combing through well-conditioned hair with a wide-toothed pick. Using Sam's comb took her the whole time he was in the shower.

When she heard the shower shut off, she thought nothing of it. Until Sam pulled open the door and came barreling out of the bathroom with nothing on but a towel—and it was on his head.

He rubbed his hair vigorously as he crossed to the dresser, a murmur indicating how good it felt to be clean again.

Her hand froze in mid-comb. She knew she should raise her eyes three feet—even two feet—but, God help her, she couldn't. He was so totally unaware of her, so natural, so graceful. Oh, hell, she might as well admit it. None of those was at the top of her list. He was so *male*. So virile. So... provocative. Arousing.

Cassie was unaware of the strangled sound that came from deep within her until Sam's gaze flew, startled, from his dresser drawer to the mirror above.

A slow grin spread across his face. "Like what you see?" She was still in his bedroom, and he liked the thought. Better yet, she was on his bed.

Cassie, who had been sitting on the edge of the mattress, still as a statue, fell backward, with one forearm thrown across her eyes.

He never left the room. A gentleman would have, but, then, Cassie had never thought of Sam as a gentleman. Well, almost, when he'd held the screen door for her—a fluke, she was now sure.

She could hear him pull on briefs, then shorts, in no apparent hurry to relieve her of her distress.

"Sorry if I embarrassed you. I'm not used to closing the door, much less worrying about who's in my bedroom when I get dressed."

Cassie was thinking he didn't sound too sorry when she felt the mattress dip beside her, next to her hip, then farther up by her head.

Memory of her almost-instantaneous response to him the night before made her shoot back up to a sitting position. She knew she should stand, but she didn't think her knees would hold her.

Reclining on one elbow, Sam lay his large hand on the bare skin of her exposed shoulder. "You're fine. Stay there."

She glanced over her shoulder at him, expecting to see wet head and chest hair, determined to act unaffected. If it didn't bother him, it shouldn't bother her.

Gone was the wild look. "You shaved," she said in genuine surprise. If she had raised her eyes earlier, she would have noticed. If she'd gone into the other room to comb out her hair, she wouldn't be groping for conversation now.

In place of several days' growth was a well-defined jaw. She should have expected it, given the rest of his body. She should have been ready for the impact, but she wasn't. Together with his large, muscular body, navy eyes, sun crinkles and perfect teeth, he was everything the wild man had hinted at. And more.

And lounging on the bed beside her.

When she remembered to move, she searched for the missing comb, only to find it dangling from a particularly nasty knot in her hair.

"Need help?" he asked from behind her.

She closed her eyes and committed his tone to memory. If she never saw Sam after today and lived to be a hundred, she'd know that quiet, gravelly voice anywhere. And he'd probably sneak up on her just as soundlessly as ever.

Cassie tugged the knot into compliance. "Nope. Just finished. Thanks." She handed him his comb, careful not to come in contact with his fingers, afraid that if she did, she'd be drawn down on the mattress toward him.

She jumped when the front screen door slammed, unsure whether she liked the distraction or hated it.

"That'll be Bill," Sam said. Rising in one, smooth, catlike motion, he ran the comb through his hair without looking in the mirror, then tossed it onto the dresser.

Cassie wondered how she could suggest he put on a shirt without sounding like a fool or like a mother. She might not be sure what her feelings were at this point, but she knew for certain they were not motherly. She followed him out of the bedroom with an assessing eye and a whole new appreciation of what lay beneath the shorts.

"Bill, I'd like you to meet—" Sam began as they all met in the tiny kitchen.

"Cassie Osbourne!" the small, gray-haired man said with a gasp.

Cassie smiled politely. So, somebody in the boonies had recognized her on sight.

"You know her?" Sam asked with a slight frown.

"Seen her on the news every hour on the hour for the past two days. You found her. I'll be damned." He rubbed a hand over his whiskered jaw as he glanced from Sam to Cassie, then paused to study Sam.

"Oh, my God." Cassie's mouth went dry. "My parents!"

"You better call 'em, Miss Osbourne. I seen them on the news, too, talking to the head of one of the search-and-rescue teams—"

"Teams? Oh, Lord, they must think I'm dead by now."

"In two days?" Sam said in disbelief.

Cassie gave a very unladylike snort. "I'm not you, Sam. I'm a city girl. And Grandpa made sure I stayed a city girl with the stories he used to tell me."

"Lots a' volunteers, too," Bill added. "Mostly from a small town. Natchoon, I think they said."

Cassie groaned. "My whole family thinks I'm dead. Could I use your phone?"

"Right in here." Bill led Cassie into the main room, to the phone by the computer.

"Wait a minute," Sam said as she picked up the receiver and started to dial.

Cassie held up her index finger to stall him, then continued dialing.

"Wait a minute." Sam pushed the button down, effectively breaking the connection.

"Sa-am!" she protested, batting his hand away.

He reached for the receiver.

She held it away and glared up at him. "What's the matter with you?"

"I'm thinking."

"Well, good for you. I'll talk quietly when I break the news to my parents that their only daughter is alive and well." She reached for the numbers again.

Sam kept the button depressed as he turned to Bill. "You say she's been on the news?"

"Every hour on the hour. Seems she's a national hero with Olympic medals an' all. They started lookin' for her before dark the first day she was missin'."

"Lots of publicity?" Sam said, thinking out loud.

"Sam," Cassie repeated in a threatening tone. "Move that finger or lose it." She waggled the hard receiver under his nose so he would understand.

Without looking, he grabbed her tiny hand in his larger one with little effort and held it to restrain her. "This is perfect." His smile grew. "Just perfect."

Cassie gave up, snatched her hand loose and plopped onto the couch. "What's perfect?" She crossed her arms over her chest, not really interested and not caring if he knew it.

"Publicity." Sam grinned.

"For my running shoes?"

Sam grimaced. "No. For the panthers."

Bill looked at the two of them as if he expected the furniture to start flying.

"You don't get it, do you?" Sam asked her.

She shook her head where it rested in frustration on the back of the couch. "You want everyone to know about that idiot panther running around out there, licking me every chance it got?"

"No, no." He moved quickly toward her.

Bill ducked out the front door. "Gotta go."

Sam perched on the arm of the couch next to her, excitement oozing out of every pore. "I want everyone to know about the endangered Florida panthers. You can tell them. You'll have the exposure they need."

"Fine," she said as she stood up, glad that he'd gotten away from the phone and said whatever he had to say. "Now may I call my parents?"

Sam grasped her hand to stall her for a moment while he thought her question through. "Sure. Tell them you're safe and sound here on my ranch. Tell them the reporters can talk to you here."

"Here?"

He nodded as his thumb idly, gently, stroked her knuckles. "You can leave after they interview you."

"I want to go home, Sam."

"Here."

"You mean, you won't let me go—"

"Of course you're free to go. If you want." He could do a mother proud with that tone meant to induce guilt in the third degree. "If you can't find it in your heart to do this for me, do it for them."

Cassie sighed. "All you had to do was ask. I'll do it, as long as they get here today."

"Oh, they'll get here. Bill's not one to exaggerate. You're hot stuff right now."

Cassie grinned down at him. "You should see me run, buddy. I'm always hot stuff." She picked up the phone. "By the way, where the hell am I?"

SAM REMEMBERED Cassie wanted pancakes and scrambled eggs, and he was more than happy to cook them for her while she gave her parents the good news and told them where she was. She repeated "Tell him I'm fine" and "Tell her I'm fine, too" time and again. And with Cassie's squeal of "She did? How much did it weigh?" he assumed someone close had given birth in her absence.

Nobody thought anything of it if Sam disappeared for days on end. Just Bill, and he wouldn't worry until the panthers started running out of food.

"Tell them I'll drive you home after the reporters leave," he called to her from the kitchen.

"They say they'll come get me."

He poked his head out the doorway. "I'd like to," he said simply, then smiled when Cassie agreed. Maybe she wouldn't want to leave immediately. He could hope.

By the time she got off the phone, her breakfast was ready. And by the time she was done raving about his cooking and stuffing herself, he was ready to further her education for the interview.

"This is Achilles," he said as they approached the first pen. Achilles was happy to bestow a lick or two on Sam's hand before strolling off to lie in the shade in his enclosure.

"Why isn't he out running loose like the other one?" He looked perfectly healthy to Cassie.

Sam grunted. "The fools that had him as a kitten decided claws were too hard on their furniture. Over here is Annie. She's too old to breed, but she makes a great surrogate mom."

He let her linger at each pen as long as she liked, taking great satisfaction in her interest, saving the best for last.

"Kittens! Oh, Sam, they're adorable. Look at those spots. Where's their mother?"

"Game commission's got her right now. She was shot by poachers. Remember Watson and his boys? It was probably them. But she'll be released soon. When I'm done bottle-raising these—" he reached in and picked up a kitten, then handed it to Cassie "—I'll give them to Annie to raise for a while."

"She'll do that?"

"Annie's a sucker for kittens. She's got a real maternal instinct."

Annie was indeed watching every move they made with the kittens in the adjoining enclosure.

"Are poachers much of a problem?"

Sam's grunt was affirmative and unhappy. "Not just to the panther population, either. They're sneaky, cagey, elusive, and the smart ones that do the most damage are damn hard to catch with the evidence. The mother of these kittens was lucky to get away. She wore a radio collar so the game commission knew by her drop in activity that she was in trouble. Here."

Cassie had to tighten her grip on the kitten when it saw the bottle Sam was trying to hand her. "I can feed it?"

Fifteen pounds of bottle-craving fur struggled against Cassie's hold.

He laughed. "You'd better."

He didn't have to explain how to feed the kitten; it handled that on its own as it grasped at the bottle with its claws and sucked noisily.

Sam watched with a smile of satisfaction. So, Cassie had a maternal instinct, too. It showed in the way she tried to snuggle the wiggly kitten, cooed at it, rubbed her chin over the soft fur on its head while its attention was centered on the only thing that mattered to it—formula.

A couple of more minutes, and she'd be hooked for life. A couple more minutes of watching her, and he'd give anything to be that kitten.

"SHE DIDN'T TELL YOU, did she?" Bill asked Sam as they put some sandwiches together in the kitchen.

Sam stood near the sink, where he could enjoy watching Cassie and the kitten romp around in the clearing. Cassie was playful, energetic. She got a kick out of watching the kitten stalk her feet. "Tell me what?" he asked distractedly as he noticed the way beams of sunlight caught in her hair, accentuating the light-strawberry-blond color when she bent and tickled the kitten's rounded tummy.

"About her factory."

"Oh, yeah, sure. Running shoes, isn't it?" He chuckled when Cassie tumbled to her knees and bowled the kitten over. "Sounds profitable."

"Are you in love or somethin'?"

That drew his attention away from the window, away from Cassie. Sam didn't like the way Bill was studying him, as if wondering when he'd been brain damaged. "Why the hell would you ask me that?"

Bill pointed out the window.

"She followed me, for chrissakes," he said defensively. "What was I supposed to do?"

Bill shrugged. "Seems funny to me you bein' friendly with a woman who's gonna tear down a couple acres of Glades to build a factory."

Sam stared at him, dumbfounded. "In the Gla— Cassie?" He glanced over his shoulder out the window, then back to Bill. "She never said it was *in* the Glades."

"What the hell did you think she was doin' in there when she got lost?"

Sam shrugged, racking his brain. He hadn't asked— not once. "Lots of people are curious..." His voice trailed off. "People wander in..."

He stared out the window. He'd been too caught up in his own business of tracking the panther to give a second thought to what she'd been doing.

"You sure about this?" he asked.

Bill nodded.

"Damn!"

Cassie was startled to hear Sam's roar through the open window. Even the kitten paused before pouncing on her running shoe again. Storming across the porch, down the steps and into the clearing, Cassie thought he looked as wild as the first time he'd turned on her and told her to go away.

"Where are you planning on building your factory?" he demanded as he towered over her. Standing with his hands on his hips, he looked ready to light a bonfire with just one spark of his hot temper.

"Sam, what's—" She noticed Bill watching from the porch, hesitant to come closer.

"Where?" he repeated. "Just tell me straight out. If you can."

Cassie stood as tall as her five-foot-six frame would allow and struggled to hold on to her own temper. "I don't like your tone."

"I don't give a damn. Answer the question."

"Sounds to me like you already know the answer."

His eyes narrowed. "You knew!"

"I don't know what you're talking about, but I don't have to stand here and listen to you yell at me."

"Are you or aren't you building in the Glades?"

"Some land just outside Natchoon has been donated," she said as calmly as she could.

"Natchoon!" He pivoted away, then pivoted back. Navy eyes had turned almost black. "Natchoon! That's practically *buried* in the Glades."

He glared down at her.

She stood her ground. Just because she was trying not to scream back at him didn't mean she had to give in.

"Well?" he demanded.

"Well what?"

"What do you have to say for yourself? You kept it a secret so I wouldn't leave you to rot in the Glades?"

"Now just one minute." She stepped forward and punched an index finger into his bare chest. "If you're done yelling, I have a couple of things I'd like to say.

"First of all, you *did* leave me. *I* followed *you*, if you remember clearly. And I damn well had to hustle to keep from being left behind.

"Second of all, it's only two acres. Two—" she had to poke him in the chest again as he started to interrupt "—measly little acres. Out of what? Thirteen thousand square miles? Give me a break, Sam. Your panthers aren't going to miss two acres."

"That's not—"

She poked him harder, forcing him back a step. "I'm not finished. I didn't keep anything secret. I didn't realize you'd have such a cow over a piece of property given to me *by a town* to build a factory that they need to put food on their tables and clothes on their kids. It's their land to give me. I figure they have the last say on what gets done with it."

Sam clenched and unclenched his jaw, then spoke slowly and distinctly. "When the reporters get here, just remember, you owe your life to a panther."

"What—"

"If he hadn't licked your leg and made you scream, you and I would never have crossed paths." He turned on his heel and stormed several yards away from her, then pivoted again and came storming back. "You'd probably still be there, dying of thirst and exposure. Unless, of course, you were fool enough to let that gator eat you first."

He stormed away again.

*That* gator? "What gator?"

He returned, in danger of wearing a path in the ground with his fury. "The one that built the nest you parked by." He noticed her blank expression. "That mound of dirt and leaves next to your Jeep? You probably thought it was a hill for sightseers," he said scathingly. "Did you think Alligator Alley was just a name dreamed up to lure tourists?"

The kitten attacked Sam's foot, and he scooped the animal up, heading for the pens to return it to its enclosure.

Cassie digested the information about the alligator nest as a chill ran up her spine. She'd almost climbed on top of it to look around.

"I already agreed to meet the reporters here, Sam," she said to his retreating back. "I understand the panthers need the publicity. They *don't* need my two acres."

"THEY'RE HERE," Bill announced.

Sam had saved one bottle and one kitten for just this moment. It hadn't even occurred to him to feel guilty about using Cassie's celebrity status to further his cause. He used whatever he had to save what he loved.

"Here you go." He handed both to her as they went out onto the porch.

Cassie accepted the squirming kitten, pulled its front paw out of the neck of her T-shirt before it completely exposed her and glanced up at Sam through partially lowered lashes.

Long, thick lashes, he noticed as he helped her tug the T-shirt up over one shoulder. A real Delilah.

"Isn't this a bit obvious?" she asked.

"All my shirts are big."

"I wasn't talking about the shirt, Sam. I mean the kitten."

He shrugged. "They say one picture's worth a thousand words."

Cassie was comfortable with reporters, had been interviewed hundreds of times under all conditions. Except these. She didn't worry about her unstyled hair or lack of makeup; she'd been seen in a lot worse condition after a hot, hard race. She didn't worry about the questions; she had nothing to hide.

She did worry about the kitten stripping her naked on the six o'clock news when it was done with its bottle and looking for adventure. In a moment of self-defense, she introduced Sam as her rescuer and handed the kitten back to him.

She'd held up her end of the bargain. Questions like "How did you survive?" were answered with replies like "Sam took time out of tracking an endangered panther to see that I was safe."

"Have you talked to your parents yet?" was answered with "Yes. I told them I'd be home as soon as I finished feeding this little guy here."

"GOOD JOB," Sam said grudgingly when the reporters had packed up and left.

Cassie snorted. "I'm sure they think I've contracted some jungle fever and turned into Jane."

He studied her for a moment as he closed the kittens' enclosure. She had done what he'd asked, used circumstances and her famous name to focus attention on the Florida panthers. "Tarzan should be so lucky."

"Yeah, well." She shrugged. "The kittens are great. If that interview helps them, it was worth looking like an idiot."

"You didn't even mention your factory."

"The interview was for you, Sam. We're even now. I'll get my own publicity later when we break ground."

In his Glades? Not without a fight. If that particular piece of land wasn't protected by law, there were other, less pleasant means of preventing what she had in mind.

"Ready to go home?" he asked tersely.

"Can't wait."

They rode in silence most of the way. There didn't seem to be any point in yelling at each other for miles and miles. They were both firmly entrenched in their own points of view.

He escorted her up her parents' front walk, though they didn't get as far as the porch before Cassie was surrounded by a dozen people and swept inside. A dozen more tried to sweep him along behind her, but he waved them off.

"Are you Mr. McCord?" An older man approached Sam near his truck after everyone else had gone into the house.

"Yes." Sam thought the man's eyes were more jade than emerald, but he knew intuitively they were those of an Osbourne. "Sam."

"I'm Dan Osbourne, Cassie's father." He held out his right hand. "I want to thank you for bringing my little girl home."

Sam obediently gripped his hand. "She's—"

"Sam!" Cassie jogged lightly across the porch and down the walk, stopping in front of him. "I forgot to say thank-you."

*Little girl?* Sam thought. He wanted to reach out and tug the shirt up on her shoulder. *Hardly.* "My pleasure. Try not to get lost anymore." Resisting the urge to touch her, he turned and walked to his truck.

"He seems like a nice man," her father said as they stood and watched Sam drive down the street.

"Sometimes," she murmured.

Dan studied his daughter. She'd brought plenty of men home over the years, all just racing buddies, she'd been quick to point out. Oh, she'd hugged them after races, kissed them even. But she'd never looked at any of them the way she'd looked at Sam.

If he wasn't mistaken, her eyes appeared a little brighter than normal.

"You feeling okay, honey?"

"Fine, Dad. I'm just glad to be home."

Her dad slipped his arm around her shoulders. "We're glad to have you home, too. I've spent years worrying about losing you in a plane crash. Your mother worries about muggers. We never thought the Glades might get you."

Cassie shivered. "You know all those stories Grandpa used to tell?"

"Yeah," he replied with a knowing smile.

"Don't laugh. They're true. The Everglades really are America's last wilderness."

LEROY WATSON, better known as Shine among his friends, kin and fellow poachers in the swamp, found a handwritten note slipped beneath the front door of his cabin.

"Junior!" he bellowed until his second son rolled out of bed and staggered into the room. "Read this here note, boy."

Junior scratched at his hairy chest. Twenty years old, and he'd always be "boy" to his daddy. He sighed and unfolded the slip of paper. "Yes!" he yelled, then hooted his pleasure.

"What's it say, boy?" Leroy demanded. Six years of schoolin' had given his son a big head, had almost ruined him.

"Remember that panther that got away from us?"

"Got away from *you,* boy. No cat gets away from me."

"They're puttin' her back, Daddy."

"What d'ya mean?"

"Game commission fixed her all up—good as new. They're gonna let 'er go back in the same area."

"When?"

"Next week."

# Chapter Six

"Cassie? It's Sam."

It wasn't that she hadn't expected him to call. She had. She'd even hoped. She wanted to see if he was as big, powerful and magnetic as she'd been imagining him all week or if her fantasies had conjured up a much larger, more virile image than actually existed.

But after spending the better part of three days with Sam, Cassie knew he wasn't the type of man to let sleeping dogs lie. He was going to pursue the issue of her building a factory where he didn't want one, and he wasn't going to let up. She would just put her foot down firmly, let him know it wasn't an option, and then, if he didn't call her again, she'd call him.

She smiled to herself; she'd never pursued a man romantically. Investors, yes. Contractors, yes. Even training partners. But none of them could hold a candle to the rough-and-tough jungle man she'd met. "Yes?"

"You remember that panther I told you about? The one shot by poachers?"

"The kittens' mother. Sure, I remember."

"The Game Commission vet's going to release her today. Would you like to go?"

Would she! But it wouldn't change her mind.

"I'd have to pick you up in about an hour."

"Sam—"

"Come on. It'll be a sight you'll never forget."

She wasn't one to let sleeping dogs lie, either. "Sam, why are you doing this?"

"Doing what?"

"Asking me to go see a panther with you when I know you'd really like to wring my neck."

"Maybe it'll change your mind."

"Sam, I'm building my factory," she said firmly. "I've been in meetings with lawyers and contractors all week—"

"I'm not against your factory, Cassie. I *want* you to build it—somewhere else. Come with me."

"Sam—"

"Afraid you'll change your mind?"

"I can't change my mind. The town donated the land." Contracts were signed. Most of the financial backers have committed.

"Then you've got nothing to lose. Come with me."

Cassie hesitated. She was interested in seeing him again, visiting his relatively civilized ranch, but to go back into the jungle? With Sam? The same Sam who'd haunted her dreams all week, made her think twice about eating a green salad and was to be given credit for the best, though longest, two days of training she'd ever had?

All week she'd remembered him with shaggy hair, stubble on his face, dressed in camouflage; his back, which he'd turned on her constantly as he'd hiked away; his gravelly voice, which purred the invitation over the phone line; and the naked man who didn't have the sense God gave him to be embarrassed in front of a woman he'd known only two days.

It might be interesting to go back into the jungle when she wasn't actually lost. "I'll be ready," she told him.

Cassie hung up the phone and turned back to her postrace breakfast.

"You're a lost cause, Cassie Osbourne," she told herself. "The man offers to take you back out into the wilderness, for God's sake, and what do you do? You jump at the chance."

She thought over the situation as she ate. After all, she had been raised to be a reasonable person, even if she wasn't acting like it at the moment.

"Maybe he's just luring you back out into the Everglades. Maybe he's going to leave you there this time. Face it—no Cassie Osbourne, no factory."

She didn't like playing devil's advocate. She knew Sam better than that.

SAM STEERED the truck carefully along an old logging trail, through water, around several alligators that had Cassie kneeling up on the seat and gripping the window frame. She really didn't want to be back on foot, especially now that she'd seen how big alligators could get when they were left alone. These monsters didn't even appear to be intimidated by a truck of steel. A nest here and there clued Cassie as to why.

Sam tried not to stare at her body bouncing around on the seat, but what the heck? As long as she was too busy to notice, why not? When he'd picked her up at her apartment, he had suggested she wear something that blended with the forest. Her concession to camouflage had been to slip on a loose, lime green crop top that scooped so low it barely covered her tangerine sports bra. Her legs were covered with skintight somethings—he really couldn't imagine what to call them—the same shade of orange with green polka dots.

It might not be much in the line of camouflage, but what he saw was mighty pleasing to the eye. Too pleasing. He dragged his gaze away and tried to think of something else.

He explained the history of the area to Cassie, noting the Indians had used the trail long before the logging companies. They were on undeveloped private property, surrounded by everything from tropical palms to hardwood oaks as they drove through swamp, forest and open meadows.

When a fallen tree blocked their progress, they left the truck and hiked. Sam took the lead.

"Sam?" Cassie was better prepared this time, grateful for the ankle-length racing skins that gave her some protection from the plethora of vines and branches. "What about the gators?"

"Just stay close to me."

He carried himself with the same natural grace she remembered as he stepped over roots and pushed branches aside—safer movements to memorize than what he had been doing in her dreams.

He was absolutely silent, while Cassie could hear herself tripping along behind him. Better for her to keep her mind on the insects and reptiles her grandpa had warned her about.

Gone was her preoccupation with poisonous snakes, replaced with a more gripping fear of being attracted to a man who, with his powerful grin, threatened to make her forget who she was and to distract her from what she wanted to do.

"You'll be safe with me," he added.

She doubted that. She had no fear for her life. Just her heart. If she got involved with this gorgeous hunk of male physique hiking in front of her, she knew she would have to choose. A week of thinking of nothing but Sam McCord had proved that he was not a man to dismiss lightly.

"I hear everyone else over to the right," Sam announced. "We'll say hello before we get situated."

A young, lean, bearded man stepped forward, a big smile glowing on his face. "McCord, glad to see you." He clasped Sam's hand and gave him a hearty slap on the shoulder. "We're just about ready to open the crate. I told everyone we had to wait for you." He indicated a group of fifteen behind him, some shouldering video cams.

Sam introduced Cassie and the Game Commission veterinarian who had saved the wild-born panther's life. "Give us a few minutes to get across the glade and into the trees, will you, Bob? I want Cassie to see this head-on."

"Head-on?" Cassie repeated faintly.

Bob smiled at her. "It'll be a sight you'll never forget."

"That's what worries me," she muttered, picturing herself as panther dinner that afternoon. This was no big kitten that Sam had hand-raised. "Are we going to climb a tree or something?"

"Panthers climb trees better than people," Sam answered patiently.

"You'll be as safe with McCord as if you were watching it on TV," Bob assured her, his admiration of Sam obvious. "If I could choose anyone in this whole world to follow into the Glades, it would be Sam McCord. He'll show you things even Mother Nature forgot."

Cassie remembered; she'd been there.

"Besides," Sam added with a wink at Cassie, "we already know you know how to deal with a panther."

"Oh?" The vet opened his mouth to ask Cassie more, when Sam took control and indicated it was time they got in position.

"You're sure head-on's a good idea, Sam?" Cassie asked as they jogged across the glade to the forest, about a hundred yards away.

"We'll have the best seats in the house. There's nothing as beautiful as watching a panther run free across a meadow."

"But right at us?"

He shrugged it off. "As soon as she knows we're here, she'll veer off."

"How do you even know she'll come this way? The clearing is surrounded by trees."

"She'll come" was all he said.

"She might just keep running for miles."

"Shh," he whispered with his finger to his lips. "Crouch down here. Panthers are sprinters. She won't be tired when she gets this far, but she'll have a lot of excitement worked out of her."

Sam watched as Cassie crouched a foot away from him.

"Here. Closer to the tree," he said softly. Funny how a week away from her had dimmed his anger. Of course, he'd spent two days getting to know her before he'd realized they were on opposing courses, one night sleeping near her, the next with her.

Cassie ignored the suggestion. If she moved any closer, she'd be right on top of him. That was no way to purge her dreams of him.

"There are no snakes here."

She was pretty sure there were no snakes twelve inches away from him, either, but she crept sideways until they were shoulder to shoulder.

"That's better. If we stay low and don't move, she'll be paying more attention to what she's leaving behind than to us."

"Okay," she whispered back.

"You're wobbling," he told her moments later.

"I'm not used to balancing like this. How much longer before they release her?"

She still smelled like fresh coconut, and he inhaled deeply. "Any minute now. Hold steady." Sam wrapped an arm around her shoulders and pulled her snugly against him for support.

Cassie couldn't breathe. She didn't want to move and alert the panther to their whereabouts. She didn't want to be held so close to Sam, to feel the heat emanating from his body.

He turned his head ever so slowly, until his lips were next to her ear. She wondered just what the heck he was up to. If he expected her to remain motionless, he'd have to behave himself.

"Look at her," he whispered as quietly as a breeze.

She felt his breath hot on her skin more than she heard the words. Turning away from the glade, she found her eyes locked with his. He grinned, then indicated with a nod that she was in danger of missing what they'd come to see. She perceived an entirely different danger, one much closer at hand. Slowly she turned back to the meadow.

Once released, the panther ran swiftly away from the vet, the reporters, all the various other people present. At first she dashed toward the east, but then took a bearing and decided to veer off right where Sam had predicted. Cassie held her breath and watched in awe as the cat's muscles alternately bunched and stretched, allowing her to run, dart and leap. Her tawny fur glistened in the sunlight as she tested muscles that had been restrained too long.

Fifty feet from their position, the panther stopped and stared. She knew they were there. Cassie wondered if she knew Sam. It was only seconds before the panther turned and trotted into the forest, giving Cassie another, less-rushed view.

"She's magnificent," she said in awe.

As an athlete, Cassie could appreciate the fine condition the animal was in. As a woman who had spent her life in the city, she could appreciate the freedom the cat exhibited. As a runner—well, she just wanted to get out there and run with her, hoping to feel some of the excitement the panther so obviously felt.

"Oh, Sam," she said on a quiet breath. Inside, she was filled with an enormous pleasure at having witnessed something so spectacular. "Thank you for bringing me here." She turned, her lips almost brushing his cheek as she found him still within an inch of touching her.

Unable to turn away when their eyes locked, Cassie was fascinated as his became an even darker hue. Unconsciously she lowered her eyelids. She knew she should stand up, move away a safe distance, put some breathing space between them. She knew he was being nice to her, friendly, expecting her to change her mind after seeing this panther. Her legs wouldn't cooperate.

Sam tightened his arm around her shoulders, lending her balance. He'd brought her here to see the panther, the mother of the kittens she'd bottle-fed. He'd brought her here because he had to see her one more time, prove to himself there was no room in his life for a woman who fit into the Glades about as well as the proverbial bull in the china shop.

He'd made a mistake. This close to her, he was tempted to chuck his plan, give her her two acres, never mention it again. That kind of insane dreaming was new to him. It was something he couldn't afford to do.

He searched for safe words, words that would neither give in to her nor start a fight. "The kittens will grow up to look just like her."

Ever so gently, Cassie pulled away. She stood up shakily and blamed her weakness on the length of time she'd been cramped in an uncustomary position. She followed his lead. "Don't they all look alike?"

He shook his head as he got to his feet beside her, still very close. With one hand, he reached out and brushed back an errant strawberry-blond wave. "With inbreeding, some of them are developing cowlicks and kinked tails. Her kittens are perfect."

Cassie sighed wistfully. "Too bad they couldn't go back with their mother." She'd seen enough Disney movies as a child to picture a mother panther racing along with one or two little spotted tykes following behind, trying to keep up, constantly distracted by all the new wonders of their world.

"Yes and no. Eventually I'll try to release them. When they're ready, and if they can make the transition. Maybe I'll even get a litter or two first."

Cassie felt him lean toward her, closing the small gap between them. Even after shutting her eyes, she sensed the heat from his body as he paused with no more than a moment of time between them, trembled as large, callused fingers skimmed her jaw. His touch was too intense, too tender, too—

Her eyes flew open. "Sam."

"Cassie," he whispered before his lips touched hers, warmth on warmth. "I've wanted to do this all week."

She was overwhelmed by all the different, intense sensations as his lips settled on hers. Her eyelids drifted downward as heat and softness and electricity all mixed together, making her wonder just what it was she was feeling. She was old enough to know about chemistry, but for the first time she learned about magnitude, about intensity, about locking her knees to keep from melting into a puddle at his feet.

"Hey, McCord!" they heard from across the glade.

Slowly, gently, Cassie pulled away. "Sounds like somebody wants you," she said, though *somebody else* is what she meant. Sam was dangerous to her very independence. He stood up to her more than any other man ever had. He wanted her to give up something for him, something too important. "Maybe we should go back."

Just as slowly, Sam straightened to his full height. "Yeah." He dragged his eyes away from her lips, but looked as though what he really wanted was to taste them again. "I guess this is a good time to get some publicity work done."

Reluctantly, but with determination, they both turned in the direction of the vet and reporters. Cassie walked beside him through the tall grass.

The silence between them made her uneasy, gave her too much time to think about what a relationship with Sam would be like. It was dangerous territory. "Do you like doing publicity?" she asked, struggling for normalcy.

"Hell, no. If it were up to me, I'd be out here three hundred sixty-five days a year." He grinned. "Bill says I'd be out here twenty-four hours a day."

"What's so amusing about that?"

He aimed that powerful grin in her direction. "Well, lately I've been thinking it'd be nice to go home in the evenings."

Cassie asked no further questions but resolved to keep her mind on racing, winning and getting that new line of Osbourne shoes on the market. She'd been toying with the name. This *by Oz* and that *by Oz*— advertising people had told her the distinctive name would help initial sales. Perhaps the racing spikes for sprinters could be called *Panthers*. Maybe the whole line could be named for Everglades animals. Or endangered species. *Condors, by Oz.* Hey, she was a responsible person. She recycled. If she could do something as simple as put a name on her shoes that would help bring endangered animals to everyone's attention, then that was good.

She was so engrossed over her new theme that it took several minutes before she noticed Sam holding court with the reporters, gently feeding them facts regarding Florida panthers and what it would take to save them.

"No doubt about it," Bob said quietly, standing next to her. "The man is good. You known him long?"

"We just met last week."

He seemed to take a second, longer look. "Is that right? Don't I know you from somewhere?"

She shrugged. "Maybe. I run a lot of races. Are you a runner?"

"Nah, I just jog a couple of times a week." He frowned. "Seems like I've seen you on TV. What's your name again?"

"Cassie Osbourne."

"Cassie..." His face fell as though he'd been mortally wounded. "Aren't you the woman who was lost last week? The one who wants to build a factory in the Everglades?''

Cassie opened her mouth to answer, but her reply was cut short.

"Osbourne?" The nearest reporter quickly turned away from Sam. "The same Osbourne who wants to build a factory here in the Everglades?" She turned back to Sam. "Mr. McCord, do you have anything to say about that? Mr. McCord?"

"Uh-oh," the vet said quietly. After flashing an apologetic glance at Sam, he turned away as though to distance himself from the ensuing fireworks.

"Cassie, does being here today have any effect on your plans to build?"

Sam wanted to hear her answer now that she'd seen how beautiful a free-running, wild panther was. He wanted to give her a chance to announce that she'd be building somewhere else, in spite of other people's plans.

"I came because Sam thought seeing a wild panther run free was a sight I shouldn't miss."

Sam didn't know whether to strangle her for not addressing the reporter's question or to grin at her noncommittal reply. Apparently his mind had been addled by that kiss they'd exchanged. It took all his concentration to remember he was supposed to be mad at her.

"Sam, how do you feel about Cassie's plans?"

"Well, I think it goes without saying that I'm completely opposed to anyone building anything in the Glades. However—" he continued more loudly as they tried to interrupt him "—however, I'm in complete support of free enterprise. Just somewhere else."

"Do you plan a fight against the proposed factory?"

He glanced down at Cassie. If the murderous look in her eyes was any indication, he knew he was in for a big one. "Definitely."

"Miss Osbourne, how do you feel about that?"

"Natchoon is full of unemployed men and women with families to feed, who want to work. I'm offering them an opportunity to do just that."

Sam scowled down at her. In lieu of a sassy retort, she glared up at him.

"As you can see, we disagree," Sam told the reporters. Now was not the time to stage an all-out war with Cassie in front of the media. There was another, more important, event to publicize. "Please remember you came here today to see a wild panther released back into her home territory. Write about what you saw. There aren't many panthers left to write about."

SAM GLARED AT CASSIE, furious that she couldn't see what was most important, furious that she hadn't seen any reason to change her mind.

"Can't you see what you'll be destroying with your factory?" His knuckles turned white on the steering wheel. "Not many people can say they've seen a wild panther run free."

"There's plenty of ro—"

"You seem to think it should just pack its bags and move a few miles to accommodate you."

She sat straight and rigid on her side of the truck, arms folded across her chest, eyes straight ahead as they followed the same track out of the swamp that had brought them in. "Two acres, Sam. Two measly acres are all I need to—"

He swerved at the last second to avoid running over an alligator. Without a seat belt, Cassie bounced against the door, arms flailing for balance.

Sam felt no remorse.

"Watch where you're driving," she snapped, resuming her ramrod-straight posture.

She was beautiful, but her narrow attitude stunk. He'd probably lie awake at night trying to figure out how he could be so attracted to and so incensed by the same woman.

"How can you be so stubborn and coldhearted?" he demanded. "You can't tell me that wasn't the most fantastic sight you've ever seen. I could see it in your eyes." He remembered what else he'd seen in her emerald green eyes as she'd leaned against him, as she'd kissed him back, but he pushed that thought aside. "There should be more of them so they can survive."

"Hey, I'm just building a factory. It's not like I shot one or something."

He groaned. "It's happened before."

"What?" The icy tone in her voice came as close to making Sam shiver as anything ever could.

"Land developers have hired poachers to clear any panthers out of their way so that no one could point a finger and scream about endangered animals."

Cassie's mouth opened and shut a couple of times before she found her voice. "You're accusing me—?"

Sam's brain registered a sudden punch to his biceps, followed by a flurry of slaps to his face, arm and
chest. "Hey—" he objected, without any effect.

She was all over the cab, it seemed, as she knelt on
the seat and pummeled his body. He wasn't hurt, but
found the situation as annoying as a swarm of blood-
thirsty mosquitoes.

"Would you quit it!" He was forced to keep his
right arm up to protect his face so he could see where
he was driving. He wanted to explain he hadn't been
accusing her at all, but it was hard to get a word in
edgewise.

"Sam McCord, you are the most despicable, un-
reasonable, stupid—" Each adjective was punctuated
with another annoying jab to his biceps.

"You're crazy, you know that?" He tried to stare
her down, but he had to duck. For a little thing, she
sure connected a lot. Even in the cramped confines of
a truck, she was as light on her knees as a boxer had
to be on his feet. Of course, it had to help that he
wasn't hitting her back.

"Not half as crazy as you, you lowdown, close-
minded, despicable—"

"You already said that." Sam brushed at her with
his arm and got his hair pulled in return.

He'd had enough. He hadn't been slapped by a
member of the opposite sex since he'd been in high
school. At that time, he'd just backed off and meta-
phorically licked his wounds. Now he considered
pushing Cassie out of the truck and leaving her to hike
her way out, though he knew he couldn't. But she

didn't know that. A good scare was just what she needed.

Cassie abruptly sat down on her side again, practically hugging the door handle.

"Are you done?" he asked, undecided whether to let down his guard.

Cassie tore her eyes away from the side window just in time to see a rabbit dash in front of the truck, followed closely by the panther in hot pursuit. "Sam!"

He swerved to the right. A large tree loomed dangerously in front of the truck. Cassie's arms shot out to protect herself as Sam slammed on the brakes.

The truck stopped with a jerk. From her new position on the floor beneath the dash, Cassie knew the tree had accomplished what the brakes couldn't. They'd come to an immediate stop.

"Yeah, I guess I'm done," she muttered.

Sam folded his arms across the top of the steering wheel, leaned forward and rested his head on them. He was thankful he'd been driving slowly, angry that he'd let himself be so distracted by such a little torpedo.

It was Cassie's fault. She'd been distracting him since the moment she'd screamed bloody murder about a little panther kiss. No matter how mad he got, no matter how he treated her, she never gave an inch. He was a big man. Not many people stood up to him, and of those who had, none had ever been a mere half his weight.

He ran a hand through his shaggy hair, tempted to pull it out. Stripping himself bald would make about as much sense as dealing with her. He'd never been so frustrated. One second he was furious with her for taking his mind off his driving. The next he admired her spunk. At this moment, he understood wild animals better than he understood himself.

Cassie slowly started to unfold herself from the floor and climb back onto the seat. "Was that her? The one the vet just released?"

"Yeah." Quickly he offered her a helping hand. "Nobody said she was the smartest panther in the Glades. I sure hope she stays off the highway and wises up to poachers."

He wasn't surprised when Cassie slapped his hand aside and got up by herself.

"That might be asking too much." She sat on the seat and brushed dirt off her legs, then massaged her left knee.

Alarm shot through Sam. His heart skipped a beat and he thought he felt his forehead break out in a sweat. "Are you all right?" He was furious with her, but her racing career meant as much to her as panthers did to him. Dedication like that he could understand. A knee injury could ruin her life.

"I'll live." She poked at it gently. "But I'd be a heck of a lot better off if you had seat belts in this relic."

He stared at the tree parked on his bumper. He'd never needed seat belts before, but, then, he'd never been driving along with an infuriating woman and not paying full attention to where he was going. Knowing she was not in need of immediate medical attention, Sam got out of the truck to inspect the damage.

He'd managed to drive several feet off the track. As a result, he had to push his way through thick undergrowth to reach the bumper.

Dents could be banged out, and he was pretty handy at engine repairs. Unfortunately there wasn't anything he could do about the broken axle. It could have been worse. He could have strangled Cassie, instead. Should have, when he'd had the chance their first night playing musical hammock.

Cassie scooted across the seat until she was situated behind the steering wheel. She leaned her head out the window. "Maybe I should drive."

Slowly, taking time to count to ten twice, Sam rounded the open door and stood next to her. Strangling still sounded like a viable alternative. Extending both arms upward and resting his hands on the edge of the roof, he let himself tower over her for effect.

"Maybe you should haul your sweet ass out of there and start walking."

"Walk? Are you nuts? I need ice, and I need it now." Cassie had contused one knee or the other often enough to know she needed an immediate ice pack. To avoid spending several days on a crutch, she needed to follow up with periodic treatment over the following forty-eight hours.

Instead she was trapped in the cab of Sam's truck without so much as a cold can of soda to hold against the injury. And he wanted her to walk!

"Well, we're not driving anywhere. And I'm sure as hell not carrying you."

She scooted back across the seat and elevated her foot on the dash, knowing that would help slow the internal bleeding, knowing it would never be enough. "My knee's hurt," she shot back.

Sam slammed the door. "Fine. Stay inside the truck unless you want to get eaten by a gator before I get back."

IT WAS TOO HOT to roll up the windows. Cassie hoped the less-than-brilliant panther wouldn't come flying through the window to land on her.

She stretched out on the seat and propped her feet up on one window frame. The less blood reached her knee, the better.

"Walk on it!" she scoffed. "The nerve of that man. He can't even drive a truck." She'd never hidden the fact that she was going to build a factory. "Where did he think I was going to build it? Downtown Miami?"

An hour later, the birds in the adjacent trees suddenly grew quiet, much as they had when she and Sam had hiked through the Everglades, invading their territory. Only those farther away continued their calls.

Perhaps rolling up the windows wouldn't be a bad idea. Getting licked once by a panther was quite enough; the second time had nearly given her heart failure. There would be no charm in a third time.

She raised her head to look out, then froze as a chill raced up her spine.

"Oh, my God." Men with rifles. "Run, you stupid panther, wherever you are." Cassie blasted the horn, ripping through the silence of the jungle.

Three men turned and stared in her direction.

"Oops," she muttered.

One took aim.

Cassie ducked beneath the dash just as a bullet cracked through the windshield and buried itself in the back of the seat.

# Chapter Seven

Cassie had honked for the panther's safety before she'd thought of her own—a big mistake, she realized as she glanced at her watch. Sam had been gone an hour—he was too far away to hear the horn, too far away to return in time even if he had heard the gunfire.

She heard what sounded like a scuffle, perhaps a slap or a punch, though she didn't want to chance getting up and looking. One bullet flying over her head and landing in the seat where she'd just been sitting was more than enough excitement for one lifetime.

"I had to, Daddy! She seen us!" a man whined.

"Damn fool. Now we got to go see if you killed her."

"Oh, don't bother," Cassie whispered. "Please."

Would Sam carry a gun in the truck? From her crouched position beneath the dash, Cassie tentatively reached one hand up, felt her way around to the glove compartment latch and opened it. She searched by touch through maps, papers, a rag, until her fingers located a cool, cylindrical object. A fat lot of good the flashlight was now. She grabbed it tightly, anyway.

Muffled footsteps approached on both sides of the truck, as though the men were stalking their prey—her, she knew without a doubt. In each window an unkempt head popped up above a long, deadly rifle barrel.

"Come on outta there."

"Uh, I'm fine here. Thank you," Cassie said as she looked up at the older man.

He wrenched open the passenger door and spat tobacco to the side. "It weren't no invitation. Get out."

Slowly she crawled up onto the seat, then scooted feet-first across the seat toward him, in no hurry to get close. Sam had been big and mysterious and unshaven. This man was heavy, ugly and smelled as if his last bath had been somewhere back in his childhood.

No one had to tell Cassie he was the father of the two younger men; they were spitting images of him. Dark-haired, dark-eyed, all three were in bad need of haircuts, shaves and toothbrushes. One hovered behind his father, while the other edged around the back of the truck; their rifles remained steadfastly pointed in the direction of Cassie's vulnerable body.

"And leave that light in there."

She paused on the seat, thought over her options. Nil. She dropped the flashlight to the bare metal floor with a clatter and left the glove compartment wide open.

Caught unexpectedly by one ankle, Cassie was roughly jerked the last few inches out of the truck. Her back scraped over the cracked edge of the vinyl seat, leaving behind a fresh strip of skin from her tender backbone area. She landed with a thud on her rear in the dirt, her lime green crop top up around her neck.

All three dirty, cold-eyed men stood over her, imprisoning her within the circle of their legs, and bickered. Cassie had never seen men look and sound so hard, so unfriendly, so gleefully evil, except in the movies.

This was no movie, no matter how much she prayed for someone to yell *Cut.* She sat frozen in place at their feet, afraid any movement on her part might get her shot.

Would they end her life quickly, or prolong her suffering?

Would they abuse her before they killed her?

The blood drained from her face. She felt nauseated and ill all over. Her whole body trembled as she huddled among three pairs of faded camouflaged pants tucked into hard-worn boots. She inched her top down while they were busy arguing with one another.

"Damn woman." Tobacco juice splattered on a nearby leaf.

"We been waitin' here for them to let that cat go for days, Daddy."

"Guess we'll have to take somethin' else for ourselves, boys."

Three pairs of eyes turned down in her direction—eyes bearing no hint of human kindness.

"Get up."

She looked up at them.

"I said *get up.*"

Slowly she rose to her feet, then pressed herself as close to the truck and as far from them as she could get, trying not to look like a cornered animal.

"Let's go." A wave of the father's rifle indicated she should start walking.

"I can't." Her voice shook. She strove to control that. "My knee."

"Walk." A rough shove from his grimy hand told her the direction she was to take.

She pointed to her knee. "I've hurt m—"

"Now," he barked. A jab from his rifle barrel affirmed that he couldn't care less about her knee.

Cassie jumped away from the prodding rifle and turned in the direction indicated. "And I thought Sam was bad," she muttered as she followed one of the younger men.

She stumbled a short while later, before they were very far from the truck, crashed into the brush, broke as many branches and twigs as she possibly could before scrambling to her feet. Let them think what they would. When Sam returned to the empty truck—she was sure he'd at least return for it if not for her—he'd be able to follow the trail she was leaving. Then again, he might not care. He'd been really mad about the factory. Furious.

Cassie faced the bad news, confirmed by the man and his boys as they talked among themselves. They were poachers.

Her grandfather had mentioned poachers as another Everglades danger, similar to gators and poisonous snakes. Worse, though, because poachers weren't territorial. They would pursue anyone who had seen them break the law, and make sure they never talked.

"Well, Grandpa," she said beneath her breath. "You mentioned poachers. You just forgot to tell me what to do about the rifles they're poking in my back."

They hiked for hours. Her knee wasn't too bad— yet. She knew it was only a matter of time before enough blood infused the joint to make movement impossible. If she was going to make a bid for her freedom, it would have to be before then.

Right now, though, that didn't seem too likely, considering that three of them had rifles in their arms and huge hunting knives and pistols on their belts.

Cassie had no idea where they were going, and didn't think she wanted to get there so fast. On her next crash into the brush, she stayed down. When the two sons dragged her up by her arms, she buckled and hung from their grasp.

"Move!"

"Stand up!"

"I need to rest, you idiots." She'd never played the whimpering female before.

Their father slowly drew his pistol and calmly pointed it at her temple.

"I guess I've rested enough."

Cassie had hoped she'd seen her last slough a week ago. These men didn't seem to share her trepidation. Of course not, she thought with disdain. Their boots were high enough to protect them from swimming snakes. With one poacher in front of her, one in back, the other slightly off to one side, she figured a lucky alligator could pick one of them off before it even saw her. That would be just the diversion she needed to escape. She splashed through the water, making enough noise for a whole troop of novices.

Half an hour in the shallow water dismayed Cassie. Sam was good, but if he had been following her trail before, this would put an end to it for sure. No one could track in water.

Where the heck was an alligator when she needed one?

SAM SPIED on the four of them from his vantage point up in a tree. He watched Cassie stumble over a root, crash into the lead man's back and trip his worthless comrade with her apparent clumsiness.

Sam knew better. He hoped. She was noisy—he'd told her that often enough—but he'd never considered her clumsy. Just the opposite. Unless her knee was injured worse than he knew.

He gripped the tree as a scuffle ensued. Sam warred with himself. They were too far away for him to help without his getting shot and killed first. If they'd been directly beneath him, he could have dropped down and taken out two. That would leave only one. Sam thought Cassie could handle one man any day.

Cassie scrambled to her feet. "You son-of-a—"

If it were anyone other than a poacher, Sam might even feel sorry for him.

"Quiet!" The oldest of the three slapped Cassie in the face.

The branch broke beneath Sam's grip, much as he would have liked to break the man's neck. Sam had brought Cassie into the Glades this time. He was responsible for her. He could read the headlines now: *Industrialist lured into wilderness by factory opponent.* Or *Factory dies, panthers hang in balance as McCord goes to jail.*

They marched out of Sam's view. Again.


"OH, MY GOD." Cassie shuddered. Back on dry land, she saw tiny, wormlike brown things clinging among her polka dots.

No one stopped. No one let her stop, and they weren't shy about using their rifle barrels to prod her along. She brushed and smacked and slid her hands down her racing skins while keeping the pace.

They laughed at her squeamishness.

Sunset approached and then they stopped. Cassie couldn't have been more grateful. Her left knee had begun to throb. And there was a heaviness in her right calf that she'd never experienced before.

A shove sent her crashing to the ground next to a tree. Thin rope was wrapped tightly, painfully around her wrists, strapping her to the trunk.

"I take back every bad thing I ever said about Sam McCord," she muttered as the poachers retired to a spot twenty feet away. "He was an angel compared with these guys."

Canteens were opened, jerky was eaten. From her post, Cassie could see that one of the poachers cut open a lime with his knife, then passed it around. One drizzled juice on his ankle, another took off his boot. He walked over to Cassie, a mean grin on his face, and stopped with his bare foot between hers.

She looked down. She shuddered as she saw what she feared was a leech between his toes.

He laughed at her revulsion.

"You're disgusting," she spit out.

He laughed harder and kicked at her shoe with the toe of his boot. She kicked out at his shin and missed, which only made him laugh harder as he returned to the others.

She wiggled her toes inside her running shoes. She would have felt a leech if she'd had one, wouldn't she? Like a big mosquito bite? Her socks and shoes felt squishy from the slough water, but nothing hurt around her toes.

Darkness fell. They made no fire. They talked quietly. Occasionally she could hear one go off alone in the trees.

She liked it better, felt safer, when all three of them were in one place.

When a broad hand snaked past her neck and clamped itself firmly over her lips, she could only think to open her mouth and bite hard. Effortlessly he pressed her head back against the tree, didn't allow her teeth to get a grip on fingers of steel.

Cassie squirmed, trying to inflict pain, to get free. Hot searing pain shot through her knee. She made little noise, not wanting to attract the attention of the others. If whichever poacher this was wanted to untie her from the tree for a little fun, fine by her. She stood a chance of disabling one, but not all three at once.

"Hold still." The low voice had a familiar trace of gravel in it.

Cassie froze, peered through the darkness to see if anyone had heard.

"Sam," she whispered against his loosened fingers. "How did—"

"Shh," he cautioned softly from his position behind her.

She could feel his warm breath on her ear. Nothing had ever felt so good.

"Untie me," she said quietly.

"How's your knee?" he asked, ignoring her request.

She hung her head. "Bad." She didn't mention that her right leg felt…funny. The heaviness in her calf had increased, as though her leg were swollen under her racing skins.

"Can you run if we need to?"

As much as she didn't want to admit it, she shook her head, defeated. Experience told her she wouldn't even be able to walk at the moment. She couldn't lie to Sam and endanger his life, too. "No way."

His fingers brushed over her cold hands. "I'm going to loosen this knot. It's too tight. I'll be nearby," he whispered, then disappeared as silently as he had come.

"Sam!" she hissed quietly.

Other than silence and night creatures, the only noise she heard was that of the snoring poachers.

Cassie rested her head against the tree and blinked back the first tears of frustration and pain she had allowed herself. "Don't let them hear you cry," she told herself.

From several feet away, Sam noticed she was still talking to herself. He shook his head, wondering what he had done wrong to get himself saddled with this woman again.

He longed to lean back against a tree and get some rest. There was much to be done. She had to have food and water. He needed some himself. The nearest, easiest source was twenty feet away.

Cassie didn't jump when she felt his hand on her lips again, though she'd been asleep. She instantly recognized Sam's familiar, clean, masculine scent. The moon had risen, allowing her to see the canteen as he reached around from behind her.

"Drink slowly. Don't choke on it." His welcome voice was quiet, familiar, comforting.

"I was afraid you weren't coming back."

He snickered. "I have this aversion to jail, which is where I'm afraid I'll end up if I don't bring you back alive. Now drink."

She drank deeply of the warm, stale water, raising her head when she'd had enough, tipping her head sideways to let her cheek brush over his forearm.

"More."

"No—"

"They're not going to give you any, Cassie. Drink all you can now."

He fed her jerky in the same manner, reaching one arm around the tree, always on guard, always hidden in case one of her captors woke up and looked around.

"Sam?"

"Hmm?"

"Untie me and let's get the hell out of here."

"Can't."

"Why not?"

"I need to know where they're headed."

"What difference does that make?" she snapped.

"Well, it's kind of hard to explain right now, but I think they're going to meet someone."

"So?" she squeaked. "All the more reason to get out of here now."

"You know, for a lady sitting in a pile of leaves and bugs, you sure are demanding."

Cassie gritted her teeth, determined not to be distracted by his obvious ploy. "Don't change the subject."

A chuckle rumbled through his chest. "Anybody ever tell you you've got a one-track mind?"

"What's the matter? You think I can't sneak out of here right behind you?"

No reply.

"Sam?"

"Cassie, please. It's vital that I know what's going on here. Can you hang on a few more hours? I'll be nearby the whole time."

She took a deep breath, trying to come to terms with the fact that Sam was here but wasn't rescuing her. "I feel like a pack animal you've just fed and watered."

"For the panthers? You know, the kittens will be living out here someday. Wouldn't you like to make it safe for them?"

"Sam—" She clamped her teeth together, unsure whether she was going to cry or scream at him. She'd been suckered in by the kitten ploy, and he knew it. "Anybody ever tell you you fight dirty?"

He grinned. "All the time."

"A couple more hours," Cassie muttered in agreement as Sam melted into the night again. "He just wants me to *tag* along with them for a couple more hours." She wiggled to get more comfortable, winced from the knifelike pain in her knee. "The man probably doesn't even know the meaning of pain. He has no feelings," she lied to make herself feel better.

Cassie talked herself to sleep. When she awoke at the first glimpse of dawn, the poachers were still snoring. Her racing skins felt too tight over her right calf, and with her hands bound, she had no means of finding out what was wrong. There was a small lump, to be sure, but it hadn't been there when she'd gotten dressed, and it didn't belong there now.

"Last chance."

"Sam!" she whispered back, startled by his return. Had he changed his mind? She glanced around. It was getting light enough for the poachers to see him if they woke up. She worried about the risk he was taking for her.

"Drink what you can. I've got to get this canteen back before they wake up."

She turned her head away from the lip, refusing to cooperate until she got what she wanted. "Sam, I don't want to stay with these men any longer. Untie me."

He sighed, letting her know he was put out with her stubbornness. "We went over this last night. Now, will you drink some of this? You're going to sweat it out faster than you'll be getting it in."

"No."

"I swear I'll pour it down your throat."

"They'll wonder how I got all wet, because there's no way I'm going to let you pour anything down my throat."

Sam sighed, resignation mixing with frustration—a feeling he'd been experiencing more and more since he'd met her. "How's your knee this morning?"

"Bad, as if you care. If you're going to change the subject, could you at least untie me so I can see what's wrong with my other leg?" She twisted her leg and held it up for inspection.

He peered over her shoulder. "Uh-oh." His warm whisper tickled a loose tendril against her slender neck.

"Uh-oh?"

He nodded.

"I don't like the sound of that. At all."

With a quick glance toward the sleeping poachers, Sam lowered himself flat on the ground, inched forward on his stomach and reached out. Slowly he peeled the stretchy leg of Cassie's racing skin up over her calf.

She was instantly diverted by his broad back, and she let her gaze wander over his muscular shoulders, down his athletic torso, down to—

"You're not gonna like the looks of it, either."

"What's wrong?" she asked distractedly.

"Nothing I can't fix."

"Whatever it is, pull it off."

He tugged her skins back down and slid backward. "You don't just pull a leech off," he growled in her ear.

"I don't care how you get it off. Just do it," she hissed.

"Don't be such a sissy."

"Sissy!?"

"Don't you know they use leeches in hospitals? They have great medicinal qualities."

She gritted her teeth and replied through tight lips, "I am not in a hospital. I am in a damn jungle with a moron who won't—"

"Careful now." He grinned. "I'm all you've got."

"And a fat lot of good you're doing me."

He inched backward, melting into the jungle.

"Sam!"

"Hush up. I'll get what you need and be right back. Unless your friends wake up first."

# Chapter Eight

The snores ended one by one as the poachers woke up, stretched and purposely kicked the unlucky one next to them.

Cassie waited for Sam to come back, fearing yet understanding that with the poachers awake, his return would be impossible. She pointedly looked anywhere but at her leg. It didn't feel like a bite. It didn't hurt. If her skins weren't so tight, she probably wouldn't have even felt it.

She was tired, dirty and disgusted. "I really can't believe this is happening to me," she said with a quiet sniffle as she rested her head back against the tree trunk. "I'm a good person. Maybe I don't go to church as often as I should..."

Soon they would start hiking again. She was going to have to attempt to walk with a badly contused knee in order to help Sam protect the panthers. She'd heal in time; a bullet would be fatal to them.

"Can you bend your leg back here?" Sam's whisper came from low on the ground behind her.

Startled, Cassie glanced back to see Sam hiding in the undergrowth behind the tree. There was more foliage covering him this morning, plucked from somewhere else to do the job. He was even difficult for her to see. The three poachers were bickering over whether to take time for a small fire and coffee.

*Limber* wasn't the word Sam would have used to describe Cassie as she bent her right leg out like a chicken wing and pushed it back toward him. He was tempted to think she was double-jointed, and grateful for it because he barely had to reach beyond the tree. The fewer chances he took now, the better able he would be to get Cassie safely away later.

In place of the canteen which he had returned, he had procured a fresh lime. He sliced it open with his knife and drizzled juice on the unlucky hitchhiker, then tugged the leg of Cassie's skins back down after it dropped off. If he moved quickly and covered his trail, he could sneak away again and the other men would never know Cassie had an ally.

"Try to stay out of trouble for a few more hours" were his parting words. He backed away as silently as he'd come. He was gone.

"Someday, Sam McCord, I'm going to break you of that disappearing act of yours," Cassie vowed into thin air. Just as soon as she'd said the words, she wondered what had possessed her ever to think she wanted to put the time or effort into such a lost cause. It would take the force of a hurricane to change Sam.

She glanced behind her, hoping Sam hadn't overheard. She had other, more important things to think about—if she ever got out of here alive. *If* Sam ever decided to help her.

But, if Sam *did* help her out of this one, she'd owe him her life—again. She'd have to give serious consideration as to how she could repay him. With poachers like these three roaming the jungle, tracking and shooting at endangered panthers, Sam needed to be spending his time protecting them, not traipsing after her.

Although this time it *was* his fault she was here in the first place.

THE YOUNGER SON approached Cassie slowly. An evil grin spread across his ugly face as he inched his hunting knife up on his belt.

"She's kinda perty, Daddy," he said over his shoulder. "If you like skinny redheads."

Cassie stared up at him, determined not to be intimidated, not to show fear. It wasn't difficult. She'd always hated being categorized as anything, including a redhead. "Skinny" was an insult she'd gotten over years ago. She took a deep, calming breath, biding her time. If he cut her loose, she'd show him what a "skinny redhead" was capable of. She knew she could handle one of them.

His brother sauntered over, his dark gaze centered on Cassie's full breasts, accentuated with each deep breath she took. "She ain't skinny where it counts, Junior." He licked his lips.

Two ruthless men, one knife. Cassie saw her advantage diminish before her eyes.

"I'm gonna cut you—" Junior sneered through yellow, tobacco-stained teeth as he leaned down toward Cassie "—loose." He laughed at his own intent to scare her to death and elbowed his brother for approval.

"What's takin' you boys so long?" their father bellowed. "Cut 'er loose and let's get a move on."

The two brothers seemed in no hurry to follow orders. Junior played with the tip of his knife, while his brother scratched himself.

"Hey, Daddy..."

Their father approached, tearing a piece of jerky off with his teeth. Cassie saw he hadn't improved any overnight, actually looked and smelled worse this early in the morning.

"I said—"

"We was just thinkin'—"

"I told you before, I do the thinkin' for all of us. Now cut 'er loose and let's go."

"But, Daddy—"

"But, Daddy, nothin'. When Raúl sees we ain't got no panther hide for him *again,* he just might be distracted by this little gal here. For a while."

"So let's not go see Raúl."

That sounded sensible to Cassie, sort of.

"Hell, boy, you're stupider 'n you look. Raúl will come find us if we don't show up. You want that?"

Cut free at last, Cassie was still unable to get to her feet. Her left knee ached when she breathed, felt as though someone were amputating it with a hot, jagged pocketknife when she moved.

"Get up."

She struggled to her feet.

"Raúl ain't gonna like this," Junior complained.

"Hell, he won't care," the other replied. "A bum leg on a woman ain't gonna stop what he'll wanna do with 'er."

Continually prodded by threats, Cassie hobbled along as well as she was able to. New respect grew in her heart for what she began to understand prisoners of war must endure.

"Where the hell are you, Sam?" she muttered.

SAM WAS miles ahead of them. If he'd gauged their course accurately, they would reach the small, well-camouflaged camp by noon. Then he'd know for sure, but he wasn't planning on waiting that long. He picked a spot and climbed a tree to wait. When the poachers reached this location, if they didn't veer off, he'd know where they were headed. He could return later, after Cassie was safely back home, to do what had to be done.

Nothing could be worse. Poachers were normally a lazy, unmotivated lot. They hunted illegally and, for the most part, their activities were sporadic.

But if there was a new demand for pelts, a new market that accepted whatever they provided without fear of getting caught by undercover game wardens, poaching could take on the allure of years past. The annihilation of panthers and alligators would be just a start. Eagles, protected waterfowl—all would fall prey.

He settled down to wait, one short mile from doom, when he saw them. "Holy—"

Four deadly silent men in full camouflage and armed to the teeth set out from the camp, headed straight for trouble.

CASSIE HOPPED ALONG, leaning on any available tree and feeling desperate. She would have fallen more than once, but having their grimy hands on her body, dragging her back to her feet, was more than she could bear. A lot of options ran through her mind at warp speed, most of which she couldn't implement unless someone along the lines of Rambo showed up.

"You know," she gasped through the pain as she leaned on a rough tree trunk for support, "Raúl's going to be really unhappy about this." At this point she'd say or try anything just to be able to stand there and rest her knee a little while.

The sons snickered.

"He won't like the way you've treated me," she added convincingly.

"You know Raúl?" Junior asked warily.

"Naw, she don't know 'im," his brother replied with a show of bravado.

"Oh, really?" She arched her eyebrows. *Their father was right. They are stupider than they look.* "I don't know Raúl? I don't know how he creeps around out here in the jungle...covered with camouflage..."

If she had accomplished anything, it was a brief rest—which was more than she was getting before she'd started talking. She struggled to remember what she had learned about the poachers before. She hadn't paid much attention, considering the fact that she'd been pressed to the ground beneath Sam's body.

"I don't know how he can pin a man to the wall with those evil eyes of his?" she continued.

They began to fidget.

Their father had a bit more intelligence. "Shut up!" He shoved her away from the tree and back onto the track. "Keep movin' and don't open your yap again."

"Sure, if—"

As he prodded her in the back with his rifle, Cassie saw Sam drop out of the tree in front of her, a murderous look on his face as he took one son in each arm. Without a moment's hesitation, in one smooth motion, she braced herself on the nearest tree and let fly with her foot.

The hollow sound of cracking skulls reverberated through the jungle as Sam slammed two heads together, then let the confused bodies slide to the ground.

"What the—" Sam stared down at the bulky body in front of Cassie. "Damn," he said with great admiration. "What'd you do to him?"

"A foot to the groin, a knee to his face . . ." Cassie shrugged and grinned up at Sam. "I guess he couldn't take it."

"Remind me not to make you mad." Sam turned his back to her, held his arms out to the side and crouched. "Get on."

This was a welcome change. "Are you sure?" she asked doubtfully. Moans came from all three on the ground. "Shouldn't we—"

"Would you just get on?" he urged in agitation, wiggling his hands as if that would get her going faster.

"What—"

Sam rose to his full height, spun on Cassie and towered over her. "I'm only going to say this once. Four more well-armed friends of theirs are less than a mile from here. If you can't run the fastest race of your life, you'd better jump on my back and hold on tight."

No further encouragement needed, Cassie straddled his waist as soon as he turned and crouched again. She was only able to wrap her right leg around him securely; her left knee was mostly inflexible.

To say she barely noticed his large hands as they spread beneath her bottom to assist her would have been lying. She shouldn't have noticed them, she knew. He was only saving her life, jogging through the jungle to increase the distance between them and danger. But she did notice. And when she occasionally slipped downward, he gripped her buttocks and boosted her back up so that her legs were settled snugly on his pelvis.

Her arms draped over his shoulders and wrapped across his broad chest, Cassie clung to Sam as he steadily and quietly covered mile after mile of root-exposed ground. His step was sure, his pace quick. She was breathless just from feeling his muscular body move smoothly beneath her.

Cassie remained silent until she saw the slough. "Oh, no, Sam—"

"What are you worried about? I'm the one in the water."

"Have you got another lime?" she asked dryly, resigned to the fact that Sam knew what he was doing and they were definitely going into the slough.

"I kept it."

They heard a couple of rifle shots behind them.

"Uh-oh."

"They must have harder heads than I thought," Sam mused. "I thought they'd be out for at least an hour." Without hesitation, he plunged into the water, quicker and more noisily than he would have on any other occasion.

Out of the corner of her eye, Cassie saw a long, dark form slide soundlessly into the slough. "Sam!" she shrieked, going rigid where she sat on his hips.

"Shh!"

"Sam—" She held on with one hand, slapped his shoulder desperately with the other.

"Don't tell them where we—"

She tugged on his hair.

She jerked his head to the right.

She pointed.

Nothing but a squeak passed her lips as she struggled to tell him quietly and calmly that there was a huge alligator underwater.

"You and your snakes," he muttered.

"Gator!" she managed to get out with a gasp in his ear.

He glanced over his shoulder at her. The terror in her eyes told him she was certain and it was close.

The poachers could be heard crashing through the jungle in pursuit, following Sam's trail.

Sam looked up. "Grab that branch," he ordered.

Cassie didn't need to be told twice. As he supported her weight, she released her hold on him to reach up with both hands and grab an overhanging branch. She found herself rising into the tree as Sam lifted her, first with his hands spanning her waist, then pushing up on her rear, finally gripping her thighs.

When Cassie was as high as he could push, Sam was quick to leap up, grab a branch and pull himself up.

"Where is it?" Cassie whispered from her perch in the tree as she stared down at the water.

The three men were getting nearer. Cassie and Sam could hear them arguing.

"Who knows? Let's go higher."

Cassie looked upward. The spreading branches would hide them nicely—if she didn't slip first and break her neck.

"Come on. I'll help you."

Sam stood on a sturdy branch and encircled Cassie in his arms as she stood in front of him. She climbed with her good leg, braced herself painfully with her stiff one, pulled with both arms, knowing he would never let her fall.

It was with great admiration that Sam watched her work her way up. He boosted her when he was able, followed closely, always lent a helping hand.

"Wait. Don't move," Sam cautioned.

"What is it? A snake?"

He grinned. "No. We're going to have to quit moving. They're getting too close." Ever so carefully, Sam

wedged himself into a semi-reclining position between two branches, then patted his lap. "Climb on."

Cassie stared at him. "I'm fine here. I won't fall."

"As usual, your bright clothes are a dead giveaway. Come here."

Cassie sighed. The poachers would be under them
within seconds. Carefully she edged across the branch
and over by Sam. "You're sure?" she asked as she
paused next to his lap.

"I'm sure."

With a deep breath for courage, she levered herself
until her hips rested in the cradle of his, careful not to
make a sudden move and injure what a man prized.
Once in position, she sat as stiff as the tree they were
in.

"Swing your feet up."

She stared at him.

"Come on," he whispered. "It's important. Really."

She might have believed him if it hadn't been for his
accompanying grin. Cautiously, she pivoted in his lap,
trying to lift some of her weight off of him while she
did so. The low, almost-inaudible groan in his chest
was evidence that she'd made too much contact.

He pulled her back down onto his chest. "Put your
feet on my legs," he instructed from somewhere just
above her ear.

Bending her right knee, she placed her foot flat on
his thigh above his knee. Her left leg stuck out over his
other knee, hanging in the air above his shin. Cassie
hoped her running shoe was dirty enough at this point
to blend with the foliage.

Sam placed one hand on her forehead, easing her head back down onto his shoulder. "Hold very still," he ordered softly.

Even if she hadn't understood the danger they were in, with her behind pressed so intimately into Sam's lap she couldn't have managed any movement other than the shallow breaths she took. One cracking branch, one twig falling to the ground would seal their doom.

"Over here, Daddy!"

On the one hand, Cassie wished she could see what was going on. On the other, she was glad she couldn't. Sam's arms moved slowly, silently, until they were wrapped snugly beneath her breasts, strapping her to him.

"They went into the water" drifted up from below.

"I'll go this way. You go that."

"Wait a minute! What's that?"

They were silent for a few seconds. Cassie squeezed her eyes tightly shut, afraid they'd been discovered, after all, afraid they'd be shot down out of the tree. Sam would take the brunt of the bullets in his back. Sam, who always protected her when it counted.

"Oh, sh—"

"Raúl," Junior said in fear and awe. "Daddy, it's Raúl. He's found us already and we don't got the skin or the woman."

Cassie didn't know which sound she heard first— the sudden surge of water or the yell. Thrashing and screams of pain and terror followed.

"Daddy!"

"Do something!"

Gunfire.

The two men kept yelling instructions over Junior's cries and violent flailing. "Get 'im!"

"I can't see 'im! Daddy!"

"Shoot!"

Cassie would remember the screams, the terror for the rest of her life. She tried to block the sounds out, struggling against Sam's powerful grip to raise her arms and put her hands over her ears.

"No," Sam whispered, his breath moving in her hair. "Don't move."

She whimpered.

"I know." He tightened his arms around, hugging her tenderly, protectively. He nuzzled the top of her head with his cheek. He hadn't lived this long in the Glades by taking foolish chances. They must be absolutely still.

Silence below.

Then a voice broke the stillness, "Daddy, he's gone."

"Stupid boy. Why didn't he shoot it when it first come up?"

With all the yelling at an end, Cassie and Sam could hear more danger. The approach of the others was audible.

"Raúl." Leroy spoke wearily.

Quiet words were followed by a guttural reply. Cassie and Sam strained to make out what was said, but Raúl apparently was used to keeping quiet.

"My son . . . a gator."

Less harsh words.

"And your panther hide. He was packin' it on his back."

Cassie frowned, inclined her head to glance up at Sam.

"I'm sorry, too, Raúl. We'll get you another one. I promise. Me 'n' my other boy here."

Cassie felt sick. A life, worthless to be sure, so recently snuffed out, so quickly dismissed by his equally worthless father.

So unlike her own parents.

The poachers dispersed within minutes. Sam made Cassie wait another fifteen before he loosened his arms. Of course it was for their safety, but he liked her cuddled the way she was. Her tight little rear was playing havoc with his libido. If only they weren't up in a tree.

Sam closed his eyes and pretended—that they weren't forty feet off the ground, that they didn't have opposing ideas about how land was supposed to be used, that they liked each other a little bit, for a little while.

"Just like that?" Cassie asked in confusion.

He'd rather she didn't talk and disturb the lines his mind was running along. He didn't know what she was asking, and at this point, he didn't really care.

"They didn't even tell the others about us."

"If they had, they would have had to admit they were bringing you as a gift in place of the panther hide—that they'd screwed up."

A gift, he imagined with a smile. He'd take Cassie as a gift. Temporarily anyway.

"But it was his son. . . ."

She was like a dog worrying a bone. "Poachers have no morals, Cassie. They use whatever they can, however they can."

Cassie shifted her hips to one side, trying to avoid the effect her body was having on Sam's. "I think it's time we go."

If she'd been careful and considerate getting on Sam's lap, she was even more careful getting off it. She reached up to a higher branch, lifted her hips clear of him, then inched aside until she was sitting on a thick limb.

Without speaking, Sam helped her climb down. He didn't have to say anything. Carefully, considerately, he remained by her side the whole way, always with a hand on her or an arm around her for safety.

Cassie needed to know he was there to keep her from falling. She didn't need the added complication of knowing she'd had a powerful physical effect on him. She was reminded that she owed him her life, and while she wouldn't pay him back *that* way, she needed to give serious thought as to how she would.

"Hop on."

Cassie studied his back as he crouched in front of her again. Gently she eased herself on, straddling his hips, resting her breasts against his powerful, masculine frame. He'd asked only one thing of her, she chastised herself. One thing was *all* he had ever asked.

Build somewhere else.

She tightened her grip as he stepped toward the slough.

"Christ! You could squeeze a man in half with leg muscles like that. Loosen up, lady."

"What about the alligator?"

"I doubt he's hungry anymore. And if you hush up, he'll never even know we're here."

Cassie would have preferred to close her eyes until they reached the other side. Instead she kept them riveted on the water, ready to warn Sam in an instant.

"Relax. I know what I'm doing. I've got time to be quiet now." He moved soundlessly through the water, disturbing not even an insect.

# Chapter Nine

For the first hour of her piggyback journey, Cassie relaxed with Sam's quiet, easy gait while she brainstormed how to pay him back. Yes, he'd brought her back into the jungle this time, but she knew it wasn't his fault she'd met up with the wrong kind of people. He did all the work for both of them, carrying them progressively toward civilization.

"You want me to walk for a while?" she asked softly, her head resting on the arm she had draped over his shoulder, her lips near his ear.

He shook his head, apparently deep in his thoughts, too.

"You want to stop and rest?" While small compared with Sam, she was no featherweight.

"No, I'm fine." He hiked on without missing a beat. "Do you?" he asked suddenly, as if the thought that she might be exhausted had just occurred to him.

She smiled. "Me? I'm not doing any work." She resisted the temptation to plant a kiss above his ear.

For the second hour, she mulled over how to approach her investors for more money. If she had more money, perhaps she could find a different piece of property. She wouldn't give up her factory, but she supposed she could make some concessions, as long as the factory remained near enough Natchoon to be worthwhile for the townspeople.

"You're awfully quiet," Sam said. "Used to be when you weren't talking to me, at least you were talking to yourself."

"Just thinking."

"Yeah. Me, too," he replied quietly.

During the first hour, Sam thanked his lucky stars that neither of them had been seriously injured or killed. His relief increased with the distance he put between them and danger.

During the second hour, his mind wandered to the woman he carried on his back. She was so small compared with him. He didn't see how she'd ever been able to beat every other woman in the world to earn four gold medals. It wasn't that he thought she didn't have muscles—he knew firsthand she was strong enough to keep up with him for days on end. It was just that she was so...delicate sometimes, so...feminine. So wonderful wrapped around him for the past two hours.

During the third hour, he tried to keep focused on the fact that he hadn't accomplished his objective yet—to change her mind about building in the Glades. If he didn't keep that foremost in his mind, he was going to be lost.

Wrapped around his hips as she was, draped over his shoulders, her full breasts scrunched beneath her sports bra and pressed against his back muscles—all that threatened his objective, if not his sanity.

"Cassie—"

"I was just thinking—"

Three hours of near silence, and they had to start at the same time.

"Go ahead," Sam offered. Better to know what she had on her mind before he started throwing his weight around. She was still vulnerable from the kidnapping, he was sure. Perhaps grateful enough to listen to reason.

"No, you."

He shifted her higher on his back. "Oh, I was just thinking of a lot of things. You first."

"Mmm." How to begin? Cassie wasn't even sure how she could do what she was considering. It all depended so much on others, on circumstances, on their finances. "Me, too. I know why you brought me here. And I want you to know I've given it a lot of thought."

Sam figured that if she still refused even to consider any alternatives, he might just dump her right there. Although it would be hard to let go of her body, to deprive his ear of the words spoken so softly nearby.

"There are so many other people involved."

The words didn't sound any different. Her tone did. He waited.

"I was thinking maybe I could go see my financial backers, my sponsors...maybe I could ask them for more money."

For what? he thought angrily. A *bigger* factory?

"If I had more money, I could look around for a different piece of property." She sensed a slight jog in his step. "It would still have to be close to Natchoon, of course. That's why I became involved in this venture in the first place. It wouldn't make sense to make people drive an hour to go to work."

"No, it wouldn't," he replied softly. *She cared.* He'd reached her. One way or another, he'd begun to get to her. He didn't care why. He didn't care if she modified her plans because she saw a beautiful, wild panther run free or because the kidnappers had scared her half to death and she never wanted to step foot near the Glades again.

This was almost too easy, he told himself, but he'd take it.

"What did you want to say, Sam?"

"Hmm? Oh, I forget."

Fortunately she was behind him and couldn't see his smile. Victory could be so sweet.

"You understand I'm not promising anything," she added. "I'm just saying I'll try."

"I understand. I'll help if you want. I can be a very convincing guy." Normally, anyway. He'd never had to crack an individual quite as stubborn as Cassie.

"I'll hound them for a month. I'll look for additional investors. I'll call every sponsor I've ever heard of. For a month," she repeated. "After that, I've got to begin building somewhere."

"I'm sure you'll get more money. Running shoes are very popular. You're famous. Knowing you, you've probably already got runners lined up to wear your shoes in Atlanta in '96. What more could they want?"

"I just don't want you mad at me in a month if they don't come through."

"Why not?"

"Why not what?"

"Why don't you want me mad at you?"

The question hung heavily between them. "Well, you've done so much for me."

"True."

"You've saved my life."

"True."

She tugged on his hair. "Hey, it's not like I haven't returned the favor."

His chuckle rumbled through his back into her chest. "What? You think I couldn't have handled that gator? Didn't you ever watch Tarzan movies?"

Tarzan when she was a child, Indiana Jones when she was an adult—Sam was both rolled together, and a nice package he made beneath her, too.

He shifted her weight higher again, splaying his hands across her buttocks and pressing her against him. She wondered if the movement was intentional.

"You still haven't answered my question," Sam reminded her.

"What?"

"Why don't you want me mad at you?"

"If you're waiting for me to say I like you, forget it."

He laughed.

"You're overbearing ... opinionated ... obsessive ..."

"You were more convincing in the truck."

"I can smack you again if it'll help. Quit laughing. Someone might be following us."

"I didn't leave a trail to follow. When I go back after those guys, I don't want them to know where I'm coming from."

"Go back?" She raised her head, no longer so relaxed.

Sam didn't reply; there was no need. Cassie understood he had to pursue the poachers before they killed a panther. She hoped he got to them before they got to him.

"I'll file a complaint with the police," she offered. "If they don't go to jail for poaching, maybe a stiff sentence for kidnapping will put them out of commission for a while."

As elusive as they were, in as large an area as they were in, Sam knew the chances of their being apprehended on a kidnapping charge were as near to nil as one could get.

If anything was to be done about the poachers, it would have to be by someone who could follow them without worrying about red tape.

CASSIE WAS THRILLED to see Sam's ranch again. George squawked and ran pigeon-toed out the screen door as they entered, barely observed by either of them. Household clutter faded into the background as Sam carried her all the way into the bathroom and set her on her feet.

"Do you need any help?" He turned and faced her, his chest bare inches away from her breasts; he was not in any hurry to put distance between them.

Cassie felt chilly, as though part of her body had been wrenched away from her. She'd been glued to Sam's back for so long he had become almost as essential to her as breathing. "Uh...no. I can manage."

"You're sure?" He indicated her knee with a nod as his hand lingered on the soft skin of her arm. "I wouldn't want you to fall or anything."

"Well, I won't say it doesn't hurt. But I can manage." He had already done more than she'd ever expected or hoped for. "I've dealt with bad knees before."

His reply was a simple nod. He knew she hadn't gotten where she was in this world by being dependent on anyone. Heck, he wouldn't be interested in her if she were dependent.

That thought startled him. How interested? he wondered. As in romantically interested? As in permanently interested?

Even she had said she'd only try for a month to do what he'd asked. She'd made no promises he could bank on.

He pointed at the closet needlessly as he backed out of the small bathroom. "Linens are in there."

"I remember."

Cassie stripped out of her running clothes, her mind on what she'd like to be doing. She'd just had her legs wrapped around the man for hours. A woman couldn't look at—much less ride on—Sam's body and not think of delicious pleasures.

She jumped as though caught in the act when Sam knocked on the door and opened it a crack.

"Did you find everything you need?"

*Need? If my needs and wants were compatible...* "I'm fine, Sam," she said, instead. "Thanks." The shower felt heavenly as she stepped in and let water cascade over her head.

"Cassie?"

She started at the nearness of his voice and a squeak escaped her lips.

"Are you all right?"

This time she didn't scramble to cover herself with spread hands or washcloth. If he suffered because of it, too bad. "I'm fine."

"I thought I heard you call."

"In your dreams." *And mine.*

Sam chuckled loud enough for her to hear him over the running water. A month, she'd said. He was sure she could do it in a month. Then they'd have no reason to be at odds with each other. They'd—he'd—have no reason to oppose her on anything.

He noticed she didn't shrink from the steamy glass shower doors the way she had on her first visit. The doors weren't as steamy, either. Though what he saw should have steamed up something.

She raised her arms, rinsed her hair, twisted it and squeezed out the excess water. He could see it all, every movement, the way her full breasts thrust up and out and moved freely, her slender waist, the darker triangle below that. Only the details were a blur, and his mind was doing a darn good job of filling those in.

His gaze leisurely roamed upward. How she ever managed to scrunch all that feminine flesh into a skintight sports bra was beyond him. How did she breathe?

"Is there enough soap?" he asked. Anything to linger.

"Yes, thank you."

The bathroom wasn't very warm, yet Sam suddenly felt very hot. He stripped his T-shirt over his head in one fluid motion, then dropped it on top of her clothing on the floor. He stared at the pile. His on hers.

Oh, God, he thought.

"Sam? Are you still there?"

He cleared his throat, guilty as charged, having difficulty controlling his breathing. "Uh, yes." He kicked his shoes into a corner and leaned against the wall, one hand on the waistband of his shorts.

"Did you find the shampoo?" he asked. He knew he'd run out of questions to ask her soon. Would he have to leave then?

Slowly Cassie slid open the tub's shower door, exposing herself to his unobstructed view.

No way he could leave now.

His mind hadn't done a fair job of filling in hidden details. He hadn't had an inkling of how beautiful, how curvy, how feminine she really was. This was worth waiting for. This was a Cassie he thought he'd never see.

He remained still as Cassie's gaze slowly flowed down his body, searing his skin without so much as a whisper of a touch. Again his eyes roamed her naked body, delighting in every hill, every valley, torturing him with want.

"Cassie..." He didn't know what to say, whether to even try. Obviously, considering where she was staring, she *knew* what he was thinking. He struggled for a coherent thought. "Need someone to do your back?"

"I thought you'd never ask," she replied softly.

He forced his eyes to begin the journey upward, tearing them from where he'd been focused. Slowly, but not too slowly; he didn't want to keep her waiting.

Cassie watched as his eyes settled on hers. His hands paused near his waistband.

"You sure?" he asked hoarsely.

She smiled, relieved by the strain in his voice.

"Well—" he began to strip off his shorts, a devilish grin spreading wide "—I *would* like to get in there before you use all the hot water."

Cassie's mouth went dry. Well-developed muscles rippled beneath tanned skin as Sam bent and pushed every stitch of clothing to the floor, then kicked all items aside.

It wasn't a hot shower he needed, she noticed, as he stood there in full need.

Cassie stood her ground as he stepped into the enclosure, letting him—making him—brush up against her. Without hesitation, he pulled her firmly against his chest, swallowed her in the circle of his arms as he rotated his body against hers, still slick from traces of soap.

She tipped her head back, welcoming the firm pressure of his lips on hers, forgetting everything but this moment as he possessed her with an electrical charge that heated her far beyond the temperature of the water.

The shower sprayed over them both, rinsing the slickness away, increasing the friction of skin on skin as he continued to move against her, tease her with fingers that fluttered down her ribs, over her hips, down even lower, then dipped between her thighs.

No longer was Cassie exhausted from her lack of sleep the night before. She knew she wouldn't be getting any sleep for a long while now, either.

No longer did her stiff knee occupy any part of her mind. She had better things to think about.

No longer did she concern herself about the factory or paying him back. This was man-woman stuff, all-encompassing, all-consuming, having nothing to do with owing anybody anything. The other issues would have to wait.

Cassie rose up on tiptoe, adding her own delicious torment to his as she ran her fingers through hair that was long and shaggy when dry, thick and sensuous when wet.

He inched her away slightly, and she discovered him staring down between their bodies. "I watched you in the forest, you know, that first time."

She could barely think, much less speak coherently. "Yes, I knew. I felt naked." No, she had felt *exposed*. There was a difference.

"Nothing moved."

She grinned. "That's what a sports bra is for."

"Maybe. But it was no fun for me."

"Sam, I saw you watching me. Anything else would have driven you over the edge." She pressed herself against him.

He groaned. "You're probably right. You don't wear those things all the time, do you?"

"Except when I'm naked."

His head dipped toward hers again. Her eyes fluttered shut in expectation as her whole body tingled.

"Guess I'll have to see you naked more often."

Her toes curled. "Sam..." she whispered, so close she could feel his breath on her face.

"Hmm?"

"Should we...shouldn't we..."

"What?" he asked when she didn't finish. He teased her lips with his own, relishing the clean, fresh scent of soap, shampoo and woman.

"Oh, hell." She ran her palms down his face, over the rough beginnings of another day without a razor, then settled her arms around his neck. "How should I know?" How could she think with him so near?

"What about your back?" he teased as his lips brushed against her ear.

"I've got a better idea."

Cassie reached for the bar of soap, sought to torture him with desire as she got up a good lather, then rubbed it back and forth over his chest. Slowly she inched her hands downward, back and forth over his beating heart, lower and lower still.

Sam stood as motionless as a statue, his hands resting on her shoulders, his eyes watching the movement of her breasts. He hadn't planned it this way. He hadn't been imaginative enough.

Her movements grew slower, more tantalizing as they approached his hard arousal. They stilled.

"Don't stop now."

"I'm afraid I haven't had much practice at this."

He drew a sharp breath as she circled him. "At what?"

"Seduction."

His chuckle was strained. "Sweetheart, you're doing just fine."

Remaining motionless was impossible as she stroked him once. Gone was any planning as he pulled her to him, cupped her firm bottom and rubbed against her to share the soap lather equally.

She laughed that light, feminine laugh he'd loved from the first time he'd ever heard it—not a snicker, not a giggle, not a titter. Pure, unadulterated female enjoyment as she threw her head back and accepted his ministrations.

"You like?" he asked.

"I like," she replied.

"How about this?" he wanted to know as his hand slid lower over her soap-slicked waist and down into her curls.

Cassie gasped. "My knees." She clutched at his shoulders for support.

Sam stopped, cursing himself quietly. "I forgot about your sore knee." He put space between them.

"No." She reached for him.

"I wouldn't do anything to hurt you, Cassie."

"My knee doesn't hurt," she whispered.

"Then what?"

"When you touch me like that—" she pushed his hand down again "—I...can't hold myself up."

Sam's chuckle was pure male at his most victorious. "Well, we can't have you falling in the shower, now can we?" His large hands spanned her waist.

Cassie thought she would never get used to Sam's strength as he effortlessly lifted her onto him and buried himself deeply in her.

Instantly Sam discovered what it was like to have his knees threaten to buckle beneath him. He turned his back to the wall for support, allowing the shower to cascade over both of them.

Groans of passion mingled with soft-spoken words of pleasure. The water beat down on their skin, unnoticed even as it turned cooler.

Sam supported Cassie's light weight with one hand, leaving the other free to roam her body and dip into secret places. He derived immeasurable pleasure from the moans emanating from deep within her throat as she was driven to complete ecstasy.

He groaned in bliss as he pushed deeper into her tight, tight body. He made his pleasure her pleasure.

Cassie gave all her trust to Sam. Trusting him to hold her up, trusting him to show her new pleasures, trusting him to take her to dizzying heights. She wasn't disappointed. In his strong arms, wrapped around his muscular body with him inside her, she experienced full release. Her pleasure grew as he kept pace with her, exploded with her, loved with her.

She nearly squeezed him in two with her strong legs. Sam hadn't known making love to an athletic woman could be so much fun, that she could give as well as she got, that they could both explode so forcefully together.

Next time, he knew, they would last longer.

She dropped her head on his broad shoulder and felt compelled to lick off tiny droplets of water.

He kissed her wet hair tenderly. He dipped his knees and turned off the water, then stepped out of the shower.

"Don't put me down. I'll collapse."

He chuckled, and she loved the way the vibrations passed through his body and into hers.

"I wouldn't dream of it." With one hand, he whipped a towel off the rack and spread it across her back. They tumbled onto the bed together, her legs still locked around him.

"Do you want to get under the covers?" he asked.

She shook her head, not wanting to move away from him. "No. We'll just pull the sheet over if we get cold later."

"Shoot, if I get cold later, I'll just pull you over on top of me."

"You're on."

CASSIE AWOKE with a start, then froze in place. *The morning after.* Waking up with someone else had never been an issue before.

In his bed, his room, his house.

Sam's breathing was deep, heavy, masculine, and came from close behind her back.

Should she wake him?

Should she let him sleep?

Sam's arm reached out from behind her, burrowed under the sheet and around her middle, eased her back until she was spooned against the hard planes of his body.

"Can't sleep?" His warm breath tickled her ear.

"Sorry. I didn't mean to wake you."

He snuggled closer and nuzzled her hair. She didn't know whether to be relieved that he seemed comfortable with the morning after or jealous. Perhaps she should just follow his lead.

"No problem. I'm a light sleeper, and I'm not used to someone else fidgeting around in my bed."

"I wasn't fidgeting." Her fingers quieted when she found herself toying with his gold pinky ring. A panther head with a diamond-chip eye, it appeared to be an integral part of his hand. She couldn't imagine him without it, didn't want to. It represented his life.

Sam's chuckle was deep and somehow cozy. "You're always fidgeting. You never hold still. It's all that energy you have. Like talking to yourself."

She thought about how he stalked silently through the swamp and crouched comfortably for endless minutes. "I guess anybody who can hold as still as long as you can would think the rest of us mortals are fidgety."

He raised up on one elbow and rolled her over onto her back. His touch was gentle and loving, as he smoothed her hair off her forehead and dropped a kiss there. It all seemed so natural, as if they'd woken up a dozen times together in the same bed.

She'd worried for nothing.

"You want me to start the coffee?" he offered, still hovering inches above her.

She fidgeted.

"What's wrong?"

"I don't drink coffee."

He raised up higher, rubbed one hand over his whiskers in a typical wake-up gesture. "What planet are you from, anyway?"

She laughed. "It's not good for you."

"You mean your energy doesn't come from *any* caffeine?" He sounded as though that alone indicated she might not be human.

"Well, maybe a bite of chocolate now and then—for the sugar."

He slid off the far side of the bed and pulled shorts out of a dresser drawer. "I guess you're a juice person?"

Should she tell him he had the most beautiful male body she'd ever seen? She'd spent years with active, athletic men. They ran together, exercised together. She'd seen it all.

But she'd never seen such a perfect body. The smooth, tanned skin on his chest emphasized well-developed pecs that had never seen a workout machine. The muscles in his arms rippled as he stretched. No wonder he'd been able to lift her and move her wherever he wanted, whether in the tree or in the shower. The man was a veritable muscle machine.

"Earth to Cassie..."

"Oh, I'm sorry. I was just..." Staring, she thought, but couldn't say it.

"Do you want some juice?" He rooted through his closet and tossed her a long T-shirt.

"I'd love some." She slipped the large navy shirt over her head.

He grinned and waited for her, his arm held out in an unspoken invitation. She snuggled under it as they walked into the kitchen, then leaned against the wall and watched as he poured her a glass of juice.

"You're staring," he teased.

"Hey, you're the one who's topless."

His eyes twinkled. "As long as you like what you see."

"What do you do to get those muscles, anyway?" she asked as she began digging through cabinets for pancake ingredients. "Wrestle panthers? Climb trees? Play Tarzan?" Picturing him in a loincloth was quite an eye-opener so early in the morning.

"Nothing so exotic. For more months than I care to think about, I've been digging postholes and stretching fencing."

"Aren't there machines that do that?"

"Oh, that would be nice—if I had the extra money."

She paused, looking at his body again, then smiled. "But not nearly so rewarding."

## Chapter Ten

Cassie sat by the computer desk in Sam's living room, tossed him a wave as he went out the door, then she spoke to her secretary on the phone. "Call everyone who's lending me money for the factory. Set up an appointment for me with each and every one of them."

"For when?"

She watched in amusement as George tugged open the screen door with his beak and sneaked inside. "The sooner the better. I'm sure they're busy and they'll put you off for a few days, but don't let them stall until next week. I've got a deadline to meet."

"All—"

"Then find that list of possible additional sources of money—the people I didn't need before—and set up appointments with them, too."

"Got—"

"Oh, yeah, and call a real estate agent and see what other property is available for building on. I need facts and figures before I start asking for money."

"Does this have anything to do with those phone calls you got following that interview on Sam's ranch?"

"No. Ignore those. Unhappy people are a fact of life. Some people are happy when I win a race, some aren't. Some people will be happy when I get this factory built, others won't."

Her secretary's tone was cautious. "Cassie, they're starting to demonstrate."

"Forget them."

"I can't. They seem ready to take on the whole town of Natchoon. They're not rational people."

"Forget them," she repeated assuringly. "Really, it'll be okay."

CASSIE WANDERED OUTSIDE and found Sam by the pens, doling out raw meat to the panthers. Beyond the small, efficient holding area stood the partially erected fence that Cassie now knew had contributed so nicely to his muscles.

Sam paused in his work and stood beside her, even dropped a light kiss on top of her head. Enthusiasm for his project was evident in his voice as he helped her visualize the end result. "When it's done, it'll be a half acre. I'll have to take down the trees along the perimeter, of course, but otherwise it'll be a much more natural setting than these pens."

"Who's the lucky one?"

He reached for the hose. "We'll see. I wish they could all have one, but it takes money."

Cassie sighed, thinking the comment also applied to racing and her factory-to-be. "Doesn't everything?"

She sat on an old stump and watched as he hosed down the walk. "Sam?"

"Hmm?"

"About money. . ."

"Yeah?" he asked warily. Now that she was safe and sound, far removed from the threat of the poachers, he could just hear her changing her mind about finding another building site. She'd start off by telling him how much time and effort and money had already gone into surveying and—

"Have you ever thought about putting on a race?"

He glanced over at her, both relieved and confused. "A what?"

"A road race."

Distracted by her unexpected question, he paused, holding a hose that streamed ineffectively in one spot. "What would I know about putting on a race? And what for?"

"Well, you were adamant about the press interviewing me here," she reminded him. "Did anything come of it? You know, like more donations or something?" She'd been so mad at him, she'd never asked exactly what he had expected the results to be.

He resumed his cleaning, turning away, lowering his voice. "Sometimes these things take time."

"I see."

It hadn't taken any time at all for Cassie to get phone calls from anonymous, incensed busybodies after the television station had aired a less-than-complimentary background report on her plans. For the first time in her life, the media had spoken less than glowingly about her accomplishments.

She lifted her feet as he hosed in her direction.

"Well, people put on road races all the time to raise money for different charities—everything from crippled children to saving the whales. You line up sponsors to donate T-shirts for the runners and walkers, then you charge an entry fee, give out trophies after the race and bank the rest."

"Sounds too simple."

"Well, I left out the parts we'll talk the track club into handling."

Sam shut off the water and wound up the hose. He'd solicited money for his panthers for too many years to think anything could be that simple or that quick. "So, why don't you do it to buy a more acceptable piece of land?"

A small doubt inched its way into her heart. Would any piece of land close enough to Natchoon for her be acceptable to him?

"Sam, I'd need five or six figures for that—I'll know exactly how much after I speak with some real estate agents. You're talking four, max. Besides, other than the people who live in Natchoon, who's going to enter a race for a factory?"

"You think people would enter a race for panthers?"

"I know they would," she said with growing excitement. He hadn't blasted the idea. "Have you ever seen a road race?"

"Can't say I have."

"People love a good cause. They show up by the thousands. They push their babies along in strollers just to participate."

His look was skeptical. "In the race?"

She nodded and let the idea sink in. "One of the track clubs in the area would help. You could have a picture of one of the panthers on the T-shirts, or a big paw print."

Sam observed Annie happily at work on her meal. Extra money would come in handy for meat and medicine, too, but he couldn't afford to gamble what he had put away for them already. "And what happens when all this money is invested and it rains?"

Cassie smiled knowingly. "Trust me, Sam. Nobody will care if it rains or if it's a hundred degrees. People can't get enough of this stuff."

"I don't know."

"It won't cost *you* anything except a little time," she said temptingly. "I can get everything started over the phone this week."

Sam stared in the direction of the unfinished fence. "How much money are we talking?"

"Enough to rent the equipment and build several half-acre pens."

"This isn't your way of getting out of your promise, is it?" He regretted the words as soon as they were out of his mouth, as he watched Cassie's demeanor change from excited to hurt.

"What do you mean?"

It was too late to take the words back. "You're not doing this instead of looking for another piece of property, are you? As a way to pay me back?"

"Sam," she said with great disappointment in her voice. Had last night meant nothing to him? "I wouldn't do that."

"And organizing a race won't take any time away from following through?"

"No." In spite of the heat, she felt cold. She felt used.

"You can't blame me for wondering."

"If you don't mind, I'd like to go now. I've got a kidnapping complaint to file with the police."

Sam knew he'd made a mistake. No one had to hit him over the head to tell him that. Gone was the warm woman who had shared his shower and his bed. Gone was the friendly look in her eyes, replaced by cold emerald stones.

Couldn't she forgive him for asking such an important question?

He watched her stiff, straight spine as she walked away, and he had his answer.

"YEP, SOUNDS LIKE OL' Shine Watson all right," Jack Kincaid, the game warden, said with a nod after Sam had related part of his story. "I haven't seen much of him and his boys lately."

"He's got one less now."

"One less what?"

"One less boy."

Kincaid sat up straighter. The two men had been acquainted for years, but Sam looked bigger and meaner today, as if the score between him and all poachers had increased considerably.

"Now, look here, McCord. Lotsa times I looked the other way while you dealt with a little poaching problem on your own. This sounds a helluva lot bigger. Just what've you been up to?"

"Not me. A gator got him yesterday."

"Yeah?" he asked with a frown. "And just where were you when this was goin' on?"

"Up in a tree."

"You seen it happen?"

"I heard it." He leaned down on the desk, toward the warden. "Every last gurgle, Kincaid. That boy is history."

Kincaid rose from his desk. "How many days you figure we'll be gone?"

"As long as it takes."

The Everglades were dangerous enough as it was. Sam wanted to be able to take Cassie back into the Glades without having to worry about her getting carted off again by half-crazed poachers.

CASSIE SLUMPED over on her desk, ignoring the newspaper and glass of juice her secretary had left for her. "I should have consulted my horoscope."

She groaned in frustration over the way the police had treated her complaint. "They acted like I went out in the jungle looking for trouble." She tossed manila folders full of financial information aside, not caring that there was no one present to hear her gripes. "And *they* acted like I was holding a hand grenade and demanding their life savings."

She sipped slowly as she slouched back in her chair and put her feet up on an open drawer. "Get started or get out," the investors had said.

"Well, Cassie, what now? Convince Sam?" she brainstormed with herself. "Convincing him has got to be easier than talking to men with their fists closed so tight on their wallets they can't get their hands out of their pockets.''

An unladylike hoot escaped. Better she concentrate on the two meetings she had left. Better she go look at some more land. She'd made him a promise, and she intended to keep it.

THE NIGHTS WERE the hardest. Sam camped out in his hammock, deserted after three days by the game warden when they had turned up absolutely nothing. Jack Kincaid figured he'd have a better chance of finding Watson and his son by staking out their tumbledown cabin.

Sam would rather have been home in bed, holding Cassie. Memories flooded in unbidden; memories of soft skin, coconut-scented strawberry-blond waves that tickled his bare shoulder when he tucked her tenderly into the curve of his body, emerald green eyes that sparked as hot as fire when she was aroused.

He smiled. It didn't matter if it was her temper that was aroused or her passions. Either one made those eyes of hers hot enough to shoot off fireworks.

"HOW MANY ARE LEFT?" Cassie asked her secretary.

"You've done everything you can," she answered as she tossed her notes onto the desk.

*Tightfisted* was an understatement for these people. Backers who had originally accepted the factory plan with great expectations were very leery of any changes that involved additional funds.

"Great," Cassie replied dejectedly as her secretary left her alone. "I've averaged 2.5 refusals a day for the past two weeks. I must be setting a new record of some kind."

She leaned back in her chair, closed her eyes and thought of Sam. She hadn't heard from him once. He should have called and apologized by now. After all, he was the one who doubted her. He was the one who had made passionate love to her all night, then turned right around in the daylight and asked if she intended to go back on her word.

*He* had a heck of a lot of nerve as far as she was concerned.

She groaned. "God, I've got it bad. How can I be so mad and so in love with the same man at the same time?"

CASSIE LAY IN BED, wondering for the thousandth time when Sam would call. She'd finally given in and phoned him, left a message on his answering machine. She said nothing about desperately wanting to hear his gravelly voice again. She said nothing about wondering what he was doing every minute of every day.

Surely he wasn't still in the jungle, trying to track two poachers through thousands of square miles of wilderness.

Surely nothing had happened to him. Her muscles tensed.

Once again, she resigned herself to a night with no sleep.

When the phone rang at midnight, she grabbed for it instantly, rolling across the mattress, tangling herself in the sheet in her hurry. She wasn't sure if she was going to be forgiving and glad to finally hear from him or mad that he'd ruined her sleep several nights in a row. "Hello?"

"Forget you ever saw us," a familiar, evil voice told her—a voice she'd heard as Leroy Watson had yanked her out of the truck. "Or else."

Cassie still had a sore, ugly bruise over her backbone, compliments of Watson's rough treatment. At least a dozen times a day, whether in a chair or driving her van, she bumped it, so that it was a constant reminder of having been kidnapped and mistreated by such a poor excuse for a human being.

"Or else what?" she snapped.

"Or else I'll come get ya. I'll feed you to the same gator that got my Junior. Maybe I'll just come get ya anyways. It's your fault he's dead."

"*My* fault!" She searched unsuccessfully for a name to call him, but couldn't think of anything low enough.

"I seen your friend, you know. He's lookin' for us. I might just feed him to the gator, too."

The connection was broken.

No different from anyone else, Cassie was susceptible to mind tricks. "Great, now I *have* to worry about you, Sam." She got up and pulled on running clothes. Eight or ten miles might help her wind down. "It was easier being mad at you."

CASSIE FLIPPED on the television in the kitchen the next morning as she poured her juice. The screen was filled with images of her Natchoon relatives, hindered by the nuts her secretary had warned her about.

"And there you have it," the commentator said, winding up her closing statement on the steps of the courthouse, clearly running out of time. "The people of Natchoon who need work now versus those who think there can be a better way."

The mayor wandered over, clearly put out with the proceedings. "Yeah, but they can't seem to state just what that better way is."

Cassie wished she'd turned on the television sooner so she could have heard the whole report.

The commentator strolled forward, away from the mayor. "This is Linda—"

The mayor kept pace. "Talk's cheap."

"Bringing you the latest news from—"

"We need jobs now."

The commentator led the cameraman away from the mayor and quickly wrapped up the report without further interruption.

"Jeez, talk about biased," Cassie grumbled, now knowing the entire commentary had obviously been antifactory. "Let the man have his say."

CASSIE OPENED her front door two days later to find Sam holding a bouquet of flowers and a bag of oranges.

"Sam!" she said in surprise. She'd expected a call— someday, maybe—not a gift-bearing visit. And not now, of all times.

He held out the oranges and grinned. "I didn't think a box of candy would be appropriate." When his overture was returned with a nervous smile, he frowned and asked, "What's wrong?"

"Oh, nothing. Thank you," she said as he plopped the bag into her arms.

He didn't know why he'd thought this would be easy. He should have known better. "Do you have a vase or something for these?"

"Oh, sure. Come on in. I'll get it."

Her taste in running clothes hadn't mellowed any. This time it was a combination of royal purple and bright orange, with a few flashes of hot pink thrown in, just in case somebody might not see her.

"You don't have much trouble with motorists, I guess," he mused aloud.

Cassie turned and looked at him to see what he was talking about, then followed his gaze down to her apparel. "Just the ones who think it's necessary to honk at every babe in tight clothing."

"Did I catch you at a bad time?"

"Well, I was on my way out." She was afraid to say where, then realized this might be just the opportunity she needed. It was certainly bound to be the only one she was going to get. "Why don't you come with me?"

"Where to?"

"Natchoon." She could show him the land intended for her factory, show him how inconsequential it was compared with the magnitude of the Everglades. "You can tell me what you've been up to while I drive."

"I'll drive," he was quick to offer.

"Did you get seat belts installed in your truck?"

"Nope."

"Then I'll drive." She grabbed her keys off the hook by the door.

"I can drive a van," he hinted.

She laughed at his ploy. "Yeah, but can you be driven by a woman, Sam? Now, that's a real test of manhood."

"I have to pass a test of my manhood?"

Cassie shrieked playfully and ducked his grab, only to be swallowed up in a bear hug.

"I thought I'd already passed that test."

Cassie looked up to find him studying her lips intently.

"What are you so fidgety about?"

"I'm not fidgety," she countered, trying to still herself.

He'd probably kill her when they got to Natchoon, but she couldn't just *assume* that without giving him a fair chance to hear her out, to see what she was going to show him. She'd drive him there in her van. He'd be stuck there with her until she got through with him. He'd have to listen to her.

"WHAT IS THIS?" Sam asked as she pulled to a stop.

"My grandfather left several parcels of land to the town when he died, to be used as they saw fit," Cassie began carefully.

He nodded, but it wasn't in agreement. "This is the piece you wanted to build on."

"That's right."

"I see you finally found it."

She laughed nervously. "Yeah, but I still haven't found the Jeep I borrowed."

Sam pointed. "Five miles that way."

*Five miles?* "That way? How can you be sure?" The area was like a maze to her.

"I'm sure."

"Right next to an alligator nest. I remember that...." Her voice trailed off.

They sat in silence for a moment that went on too long.

"What I'm not sure of is why you brought me here today."

Cassie sighed, her exhalation sounding too loud in the strained silence between them. This was it, the moment she'd been dreading since her final financial meeting. She stared out the windshield. Her voice was barely above a whisper. "I tried, Sam. I really tried."

He looked away from her, out the side window.

"I met with every banker I could reach, every investor I already have, every sponsor I've ever—"

In one swift movement, Sam wrenched open the door and stepped onto familiar territory.

"Sam—"

"You tried?" he bellowed, pacing back and forth before slamming the door with body-shaking force.

Cassie sat very still, absorbing his anger through the rocking van.

"You tried?" he repeated in a deadly whisper through the open window. "You don't know the meaning of the word."

"Sam... Where are you going, Sam?" Cassie slid out her side of the van, jogging after him.

He shook her hand off his arm impatiently. "Home. It seems I have some organizing to do."

"Sam..." She followed, on the verge of tears. How could she let him go like this?

He turned on her, looking as mean and wild and large as the first time she'd met him. The Sam she had grown to know and love was gone, replaced by the hermit maniac.

"Go back to your van," he growled as he towered over her, "back to your apartment...back to your racing. You don't belong here."

The Sam who was warm and caring and protective was through with her. Done. Finished—as if it never had been.

"Sam—" She reached out for him, touched his arm again. She wanted to explain how hard she had tried, how many calls she had made, how many meetings had ended negatively. She had to make him understand.

He shrugged her off again, cutting off any speech she might have thought of. "Don't follow me. I won't wait for you. And, lady, believe me, I *can* lose you."

Cassie watched in disbelief as he disappeared into the jungle, the parting foliage swallowing him almost instantly as if he had never been there.

She made no attempt to stop the hot tears that streamed down her cheeks, burning a trail on her skin as painful as the tear in her heart.

## Chapter Eleven

Cassie glanced at her glow-in-the-dark watch as she drove home on Alligator Alley. Eleven o'clock. For such an adventurous name, she thought the highway ought to be less boring, even late at night.

She was making good time, considering how slow the awards ceremony had gone after the road race. The check was tucked safely in her gear bag.

"So, what to do with the money?" she asked herself, tired of watching the road slip by. "Oh, I don't know. Let's see . . . Lawyer's fees?"

She laughed at the preposterous thought. "No, definitely not that."

After improving her own physical condition following Sam around the jungle, Cassie had decided to open a small training camp based in Natchoon. Several residents had already agreed to board runners, eagerly looking forward to new blood and new money. Others had volunteered to mark the existing tracks and trails so no one would get lost.

"How about a hot tub?" A smile broke out across

her face. "Yes! What's a training camp without a hot tub?"

Traffic slowed ahead. Two cars in front of Cassie hit their brakes, their red taillights glowing brilliantly. Everyone ahead of them drove on at full speed.

"Must have a flat or something."

When the first car stopped, a man jumped out and ran to the side of the road. The passengers in the second car followed suit.

Cassie tried to watch both the highway and the action, then she caught sight of something moving on the side of the road. She had a first-aid kit in her gear bag. Easing past the two vehicles, she pulled over.

Another car pulled over and people jumped out. "They hit something" she heard them say. "It looks like an big animal."

A shiver chased up and down Cassie's whole body. She threw the van into Park and slid out, her mind faraway on something Sam had said. A horn blared as a car zoomed by within a few feet of her, but Cassie ignored it as she ran back to the animal.

A small circle of people stood around the still form of a battered and bloody panther.

"Oh, my God," Cassie said with a gasp, remembering how Sam had hoped that a panther shot by a poacher would be smart enough to avoid traffic. This one hadn't been. The fact that it wore no radio collar made her wonder if it was one Sam had raised, possibly the overly friendly one that had licked her twice.

"Somebody get a gun and put it out of its misery," a man ordered.

"No!" Cassie nearly screamed, distraught that someone might heed his order. Fewer than fifty left in the entire state, maybe as few as thirty, and this guy wanted to do away with it before they knew if it could be saved. "No, you can't do that," she continued a bit more rationally, as no one had immediately whipped out a gun. "We need a vet."

"Lady, no vet's gonna run out here to save a wild cat."

"Well, nobody's gonna shoot it, either," she snapped back at him. "Not while I'm here."

"Hell, then, you handle it." He got into his car and sped off, burning rubber.

"Do you have a car phone?" Cassie asked the remaining bystanders.

They shook their heads. "You know about panthers?" one asked.

"I know who can help this one—if I can reach him in time." She looked around desperately. It was dark. Cars sped by on the highway. No police in sight. No car phone.

Cassie ran back to her van, grabbed her bag, whipped out a white towel, then jumped up and down, back and forth. They'd see her in their headlights.

"She's crazy" was the general consensus.

Several cars slowed and rolled down their windows as they approached.

"Are you nuts?"

"Get outta the road, woman!"

"Crazy people. Of all the—"

Of everyone she inquired, "Do you have a car phone? There's an emergency. Do you have a car phone?'' She flitted from car to car, van to truck, like a bee looking for the best flower, slowing traffic almost to a standstill. "Do you have a car phone?" People pulled over to the side, curious but unable to help.

Finally a pickup truck stopped. "Yeah, I got a phone."

Without hesitation, Cassie jumped up on his running board. "Let me use it. There's an emergency here."

He glanced in his rearview mirror. "Let me pull over first."

"Give me the phone!"

If she hadn't been clinging to his truck, he'd probably have rolled up his window and driven away. As it was, he was stuck with her and handed her the phone.

"How do you use this thing?" she demanded in frustration.

"Dial, then push the Send button."

"Sam?" She clung to the door of the truck and started talking the second he answered, oblivious to the driver slowly maneuvering his way off the road. "There's a panther out here on Alligator Alley. It's just been hit. Just now. It's still alive."

"Where are you?"

Cassie glanced around. It was dark. There were no distinguishing landmarks. "Where are we?"

The man in the truck made his best guess.

"I'll be right there."

The phone went dead.

"Thank you." Cassie gave the man his phone back. "Thanks for stopping." She jumped back down off the truck and jogged over to the panther, now surrounded by a small crowd. "How's he doing?" she asked.

"He hasn't moved. He's bleedin' a lot, too."

Without hesitation, Cassie crouched beside the large cat. She touched him gingerly. He didn't move. She touched him some more, harder, poking him near the withers. He still didn't move. The towel in her hand made a fine compress, and she folded it up and pressed it to the bloody spot on the animal's side. She used another to wrap the bloody foreleg.

The panther twitched.

With a start, Cassie jumped backward from her crouched position to her feet and stood frozen to the spot for a minute, unsure whether to run or stay, aware that a wild animal could do a lot of damage to a human body in a short time. The panther had claws and teeth. She had nothing but her wits.

"It's okay," Cassie said a moment later, to no one in particular. She didn't want the gun idea to take root again. "He's still unconscious."

"Maybe you should tie his legs together in case he wakes up," someone suggested.

Cassie looked at the bloody, towel-wrapped foreleg. "I think not."

SAM MADE ONE CALL before he left the ranch. He gave Bob at the Game Commission the location of the injured panther, then flew down the highway with a few emergency supplies in his truck. All the while, he knew the animal was within traveling range of the young male he had raised and released—the one he had been tracking when he'd found Cassie.

Thank heavens she'd called him. He didn't know how long the panther had been injured or how extensively. He did know that time could make all the difference.

He had no trouble finding the right spot. His truck slid to a stop among dozens of vehicles parked along the shoulder.

"Over here, Sam."

He ran, carrying his first-aid equipment, guided in the right direction by her voice. "How long has it been?" were the first words out of his mouth.

"Seems like an hour."

"No, just twenty minutes," someone else answered.

Sam was quick and efficient in his assessment of the injured animal, gentle yet thorough as he knelt beside it. It wasn't his young male, but a more mature one that had somehow eluded the Game Commission— possibly possessing DNA with enough genetic variation to enhance his breeding program.

"We've got a chance," he said finally. "Good job with the towels. The helicopter should be here any minute."

Cassie smiled up at him as she heard its approach, and he saw relief wash over her face.

"There's not going to be enough room to land unless someone stops traffic," Sam announced as he rose to his full height, looking at several men in particular.

"Okay," Cassie replied.

"Not you," he growled, grabbing her arm as she rose to run out onto the highway. "Them."

Traffic was brought to a standstill, enabling Bob to land, then conduct his own quick assessment while he listened attentively to Sam.

"Let's get him on board quickly. I've got the operating room standing by."

"We need one more man," Sam announced. "You." He selected a volunteer without hesitation.

Once the panther was loaded onto the helicopter and the volunteer dismissed, Sam remembered Cassie. She'd called him. She'd saved this panther. He glanced around quickly, knowing they were short on time, and discovered her standing back, away from the noise and wind of the chopper, watching.

"You coming?" he yelled, and held out his hand so there'd be no misunderstanding.

He watched her hopeful look, her excitement and doubt as she warred within herself. Then, she grabbed her bag, placed her blood-smeared hand in his and boarded the helicopter.

THE PANTHER LAY on the table under the bright surgical lights. Cassie reached out tentatively and ever so gently put her hand on the motionless head. Other than road grit, the fur was soft, begging to be smoothed and petted.

Sam knew exactly how she felt. He remembered touching his first panther as a child, one his father had tried to save. Technology hadn't been the same then. People hadn't felt the same, hadn't known. Only his dad and him. And in the long run they hadn't been enough.

"Beautiful, isn't he?" Sam whispered reverently.

"Yes."

Bob was finished with him for the evening. "He should make it fine if we can get him to eat over the next couple of weeks. You did good work out there, Cassie."

"Thanks."

"Can I borrow a truck?" Sam asked. Cassie had gotten the job done and saved this panther's life. He owed her for that. "I'd like to see Cassie gets home okay."

"Sure. You can crash at my place if you want."

The stars were out in full force, the air still and comfortable. It was hard to believe one of the few remaining wild panthers was inside fighting for its life on such a peaceful night, in such an alien environment.

"It's after midnight." Sam gazed down at Cassie with fond memories of other nights. From hammock to truck to his bed, he never got much sleep when she was around. When he did sleep, his dreams were often of her, sometimes fighting, other times loving, always true to herself—a trait he admired immensely.

Cassie quietly strolled beside him to the parking lot, comfortable with what she had done that night, comfortable with Sam next to her again. The fact that he had thought of her before the helicopter had taken off helped ease the strain she had been under since he'd turned his back on her two weeks ago. He didn't hate her.

Neither of them was in a hurry. The tension of the past two hours had earned them a rest, time to chat amiably.

"Looks like a race day." He gestured toward her warm-up suit, blocked in cherry red and emerald green. For some reason, on her the combination worked.

She nodded.

"I hope you can get the blood out."

"Doesn't matter." She shrugged. "People will just think I'm an ax murderer and get out of my way."

He laughed, not so much at what she said but in relief at her sense of priorities. "I guess your knee's well. How'd you do?"

"I won the ten-K."

They continued on toward the parking lot, where Sam would borrow one of the Game Commission trucks.

His grin was lopsided. "You haven't snapped my head off."

Cassie laughed that laugh he'd grown to love. Light, airy, honest. "I'm glad to see you found your way home all right."

He shrugged. "Sure. Why not?"

"Well, I didn't worry about you not having food. But you weren't carrying a canteen when you left."

"You were worried?"

"I didn't say that."

It seemed so natural to slip his arm around her shoulders and give her a light, friendly squeeze. "You didn't have to." If only they weren't always at odds with each other. If only she weren't planning on building in the Glades.

His plan had been to introduce her to a panther kitten and teach her to love it. It had paid off, even if in a different way than he'd planned. She'd rescued a full-grown, breeding-age adult. Saved its life.

He held the passenger door for her and noticed she automatically reached for the seat belt.

Sam thought about what he wanted out of life and where she might fit in if things were different. She loved little kittens, ignored blood on her hands in favor of saving a life and possessed the ability to be really dedicated to a goal.

What more could he want in a woman?

Well, that was easy. She was gorgeous and sexy, too, but if he continued thinking along those lines while they drove through the night, he'd be wanting to stop at a motel.

Leaving Cassie at her van was the hardest thing Sam had ever done. In the glow of the mooonlight, he saw the same wants and needs in her that had been plaguing him. He also saw the same hurt and confusion over their chosen paths.

"Thanks for the ride," she said simply.

"Thank you—for the panther."

She inserted her key in the lock. "I've got some juice in the cooler, if you'd like some before you go...." It was a long drive back.

He hesitated. "I'd better not. Good night."

"Good night, Sam."

He walked away from her, without the feeling of satisfaction he'd gotten every time he'd walked away from her in the jungle.

She wasn't against panthers. He wasn't against factories.

Were two acres a fair trade for one panther's life—the one she'd saved tonight?

Breezing down the highway moments later, he banged his hand on the steering wheel in frustration. It was the principle of the thing. First two acres here, then two acres there. When would it stop?

He owed her, he thought again for the dozenth time since they'd loaded the panther on board the helicopter.

At 7:00 a.m. he began making his own phone calls. He would have started in the middle of the night, but he figured that when asking people for favors, it wasn't a good idea to get them out of bed before sunrise.

CASSIE HAD HAD IT with both the poachers and the police. One kept calling, even when she changed her phone number; the other was no help.

As a last resort, she bought a whistle.

It didn't stop the poacher from calling, but it did stop him from talking. The phone rang every night, several times each night.

Then the calls stopped coming.

CASSIE CALLED BOB at the Game Commission clinic every day to see how the panther was doing.

"He's not eating," Bob said for the seventh day in a row.

"It's been over a week. He must be skin and bone." Cassie was dismayed. She didn't want to think she'd saved its life so it could slowly starve. Surely they could do something.

"It's not that unusual in a case like this."

"Can I come visit?" she asked impulsively.

"Sure. Why not? Why don't you come in the evening when it's quieter around here."

Cassie arrived late the following day. Bob took her hand in a warm greeting.

"Good timing," he said. "McCord's getting him to eat now."

"Sam's here?" Cassie asked, wondering if Bob had maneuvered this meeting somehow.

"You bet. Every time we face a problem like this, or half a dozen others, he pulls us through. There's nothing he can't do with panthers. Come and watch."

Cassie followed him slowly. Would Sam think she'd finagled this visit just to see him again? Was he here at this time just to see her again?

The clinic was spotless. Sam was crouched next to a pen constructed of cement block and chain link, making soft panther noises at the injured male, tempting him with a large chunk of raw meat on a stick.

"How's it going?" Bob asked.

"Four pounds down the hatch," Sam replied, his full attention on the cat.

Bob beamed. "Four pounds? That's terrific."

The panther wasn't as close to skin and bone as Cassie had thought he'd be after not eating for a week. Certainly not as close as she'd be if she got hit by a car and quit eating.

The panther alternately licked the heavy bandage on his foreleg and pulled at an edge of the wrapping with his teeth, his eyes never leaving them.

"How do you handle him to change the bandage?" Cassie asked.

Sam turned then, and Cassie saw she had not been expected, though he covered his surprise.

"Unfortunately, we have to anesthetize him," Bob explained. "That's what we're up against when we work with a wild animal like this. It's the only safe way, for him and for us. We don't have to take the bandage off—he does that first. Then we dart him— thanks to Sam we can drug his meat next time—clean the wound, administer antibiotics and give him a new wrap."

"God, he's beautiful." Since Cassie had seen him last, he'd been cleaned up, blood and road grit removed.

"He's full, Bob. Let's let him sleep on it. Try it again tomorrow. If he doesn't eat for you, I'll come back."

Bob gave Cassie a tour of the clinic, which housed several species of sick and injured animals, while Sam patiently followed them around until they were finished.

"I'll walk you to your van," Sam offered.

Cassie looked up and studied Sam's profile as they walked side by side to the parking lot. A breeze ruffled his hair. He brushed it back with one hand, and she remembered the tenderness with which that hand had touched her.

"I hope you don't get mad. I've made some calls," Sam said as he studied the star-studded sky.

"What kind of calls?"

"I've met a lot of people over the years. Some of them have connections."

Cassie frowned. "Sam, what are you getting at? Is this your way of telling me you're torpedoing my factory?"

"No!" His attention quickly centered on her. "No, not at all. Just the opposite. I'm trying to find you another piece of property."

"Oh. Sam, I think—"

"Now, before you say anything, hear me out."

"Sam—"

His fingers came to rest lightly on her lips. "Shh," he said quietly. "I know you tried. I know things are heating up in Natchoon. Now let me try. I just can't let you go without giving it my best shot, too."

"Let me go?"

Her words were so soft he barely heard her, but he knew what she'd said by the warm look in her eyes.

"Cassie . . . I've missed you."

She blinked back the moisture. "Me, too, Sam."

"I want to work this thing out between us."

"Me, too."

"I want to see you again."

"You mean—"

"I mean I'd like to see you again. I could go running with you. Or you could come out and picnic with me and the kittens." He shrugged. "Whatever."

"I don't know what to say. We still—"

"Cassie, I . . ." His head dipped lower as his hands rose to her face. "I've missed you."

His lips were warm and tender, full of affection and promise and memory.

"I've missed you, too," she whispered as he feathered kisses from one corner of her mouth to the other. "So much."

"Can I call you?"

She nodded against his cheek.

"It'll be a couple of days. I've got another lead on the poachers I want to follow up on before it's too late."

"Promise me you'll be careful."

"I promise."

# *Chapter Twelve*

"Cassie? Sam."

She smiled. She knew who it was. Ten years could have gone by and she'd know who it was. "I wish those poachers would disappear off the face of the Earth so I wouldn't have to worry about you."

"It's only been three days."

"Sam, I know better than anyone what they're capable of. They threatened to feed you to the alligators."

"They what? When?"

"Oh, they—he—called here."

"When?"

She stalled for time, unsure how much to relate to him.

"Cassie."

"A lot, at night."

"Why didn't you tell me?" he demanded.

"I called the police. I changed my number, but even that didn't work, so I changed it back."

"I don't think he'll be phoning anymore. Will you—"

"Why? What happened?"

Sam chuckled. "Let's just say what goes around comes around."

"Sam—"

"All right, all right. Watson and his boy—" he chose his words carefully "—apparently did some things that caused their 'friends' to suspect they'd been cheated."

Cassie was quick to hear what Sam didn't say. "'Apparently'?"

"Yes. It looked that way to me."

"Where are they?"

"Well, that's the funny thing. They seem to have disappeared off the face of the Earth."

"Sam, you didn't—"

"I didn't do anything I'd be ashamed to tell my mother about."

Cassie wasn't sure just what kind of person his mother was. Ma Barker had been a mother, too. "But you can't tell me?"

"Someday. Today I'm calling to invite you out here to visit the panther you saved. Bob thinks he'll recuperate better away from the artificial environment of the clinic. He's delivering him tomorrow morning."

"I'd love to come. What time?"

"For dinner tonight."

Cassie paused at the unexpected invitation. "Dinner?" she repeated, hoping she'd heard correctly.

"Yes."

Last time they'd been together, he'd asked her for more time while he tried his connections. She didn't have much time to give him. Deadlines were approaching rapidly. People were counting on her.

She'd give him what she had. "I'll be there."

Sam hung up the phone. As his eyes roamed the disaster he called home, he knew he was in trouble. Big trouble. What woman in her right mind would want to make love in a dump like this? Again? Last time had been different. This time he had some work to do.

CASSIE DITHERED over what to take for the night. Should she pack light and make it all seem casual or pack so she'd have anything she needed for any possible contingency? Toothbrush, sure. But what about a nightgown? A T-shirt? Chances were, she wouldn't wear either, but then again, she might need something. She had less difficulty packing for a road race, when she didn't know a day or two ahead of time if it was going to be hot and sunny, rainy or cold.

This time she didn't need extra clothes, a cooler with proper food, or a thermos full of juice. What she did need, she had to stop by a store and get.

Before Cassie arrived at Sam's ranch at five o'clock, she'd almost changed her mind. Actually, she had changed her mind—several times. Back and forth. Spending the night with Sam wouldn't resolve anything. It would only complicate matters.

She couldn't resist him. She'd figure something out; she always did. That's how she'd gotten this far.

"Cassie!" Sam called from the direction of the pens.

She felt a sudden surge of shyness, knowing that by coming here now she was committed to spending the night. Not that she didn't want to; she did. But she'd never blatantly planned it before. Although if she'd met a man like Sam before, she might have.

He met her halfway across the yard, sensing her mood the closer he got. No one had to hit him over the head with a two-by-four to tell him Cassie didn't get involved unless she was serious. It appeared from the look on her face that she was torn between caution and acting as though nothing out of the ordinary was going on between the two of them.

He chose safe territory, reached out and engulfed her soft hand in his. "The new pen's finished," he said with a tug in that direction.

Together they walked down to the new half-acre pen, which was finally completely landscaped and fenced. He felt her fingers relax in his.

"I got everything started on the road race we talked about," Cassie informed him. "They want to talk to you personally, to make sure you're committed."

"No problem."

Cassie could barely see Achilles, but he bounded over as soon as Sam called out to him.

"You can put your hand up to the fence if you want. Like this. Keep it flat—don't let him get your fingers."

Cassie imitated him. Achilles licked the back of her hand with his rough tongue. It was the third time she'd been licked by a full-grown panther, and she was getting to like it. "He's sweet."

"Don't be fooled. He and I have an unusual relationship, and that could all change as he gets older."

As Achilles got his fill of licking salt off their skin, he wandered away. There were enough trees and brush in the middle of the area to make even a wild panther feel right at home. He could lie in the shade, climb the boughs, pounce on anything foolish enough to squeeze under the chain link.

"I thought the new panther would get this pen, since he's used to so much area."

"He still needs to be confined somewhat. Maybe when he's healed a little more I can switch the two. If one of the females gets interested, they can share."

"How will you know?"

"Believe me, she'll let me know, and she won't be quiet about it. Come on, the lasagna should be ready."

"Race you to the kitchen." She sprinted off before he could react, teasing as she went. "Come on, slowpoke."

She waited for him on the porch, and got a bear hug for doing so.

"If I'd known you love lasagna so much, I'd have cooked it for you weeks ago."

"If I'd known you could cook—something other than rabbit on a stick, of course, or breakfast—I'd have camped on your doorstep."

He released her only far enough that he could hold her eyes with his. "I would have liked that." He lowered his head as his eyes closed. His lips unerringly found their way to hers. With one hand low on her back, he pressed her to him. "Maybe we should let it bake for another hour or so."

She smiled and gently pushed away with both hands flat on his broad chest. "I think not."

Amused by her reaction, he held the screen door open while she ducked beneath his arm and went into the house. "Never let it be said I starved a woman."

Cassie came to a dead stop just inside the door. Sam ran into her, and it felt good. So good that his arms just naturally wrapped themselves around her, crossing over her full breasts. He wanted to run into her more often.

"What happened to your house?"

"Spring-cleaning." Her hair tickled his nose.

She glanced up over her shoulder at him. "By yourself?"

"Do you know anyone else who would have helped?" He turned and flipped the new latch on the screen door. "George," he explained with a boyish grin. "He's been eyeing the computer lately."

Cassie was impressed. She didn't know if a man had ever cleaned house for her before, but it was obvious that Sam had taken both the time and trouble to do so. "I'm glad you left all the photos up."

"I found some more. They're in the kitchen."

She followed him, to find the wall and cabinets covered in an artistic display. "You must have had a drawerful somewhere."

He perused the photos with a loving eye. "That's Achilles." He nodded toward a collage arranged on the cabinet that held the glasses. "He was just losing his spots when I got him."

"It's a shame he was declawed."

"Well, yes and no. With his DNA, we really need him in captivity as a breeding male."

The kitchen table was already set for two, with a flowered cloth and plain dishes. Two candles set off to one side. Sam turned off the overhead light and instantly changed the mood from kitchen to private dining nook.

He opened the oven and retrieved the lasagna. "What would you like to drink? Iced tea?"

"Sounds good. I'll get it."

"I've got salad in the fridge, too."

They met back at the table. She felt silly having a man hold her chair for her when she was wearing shorts and a tank top, but took the gesture in the manner it was intended.

No sooner had Sam sat across from her than Cassie heard something scream outside. "What the..." She was on the edge of her chair, ready to jump up and run out to see what was being killed.

"What?" Sam asked.

"Didn't you hear that?" She couldn't believe he wasn't already on his way out the door with a gun in his hand. Something horrible was out there.

He shrugged. "I didn't hear anything unusual. What did it sound like?"

She twisted her napkin as she struggled for the right description. "I don't know. It reminded me of when my dad used to watch Westerns on TV and there would be a scream at night."

"Oh. Mountain lions." He heaped steaming lasagna onto her plate.

"Yeah," she agreed, relieved she'd explained herself so well. Then she realized that the cats he had outside belonged to the same general breed. "Oh. Do they do that all the time?"

"Most nights. Achilles is probably just checking to make sure everyone else is still there."

Dinner was punctuated with several screams that evening. Cassie never got used to them—she loved and appreciated the beauty of every one.

"This is absolutely fabulous," she said.

He smiled proudly. "I'm glad you like it."

She laughed nervously. "I'm sorry. Your cooking is great, too, but I meant the panthers. I can't believe I'm sitting here calmly eating dinner and listening to them screaming out there in your yard. It's like...I don't know...I feel honored somehow. Do you know what I mean?"

"Every day." He reached across the table and took her hand in his.

Candlelight flickered as they finished dinner and cleaned up. Electricity crackled between them when she returned to his side.

Ahh, how he loved her by his side.

Sam turned away from the sink, reached out and tugged on the towel she held, pulling her gently, firmly, slowly toward him. "I have strawberry short-cake for dessert," he offered, hoping she'd refuse.

"Mmm. I thought I saw strawberries in the fridge." Slowly she turned away from him.

He followed closely, intending to distract her as much as possible.

Cassie opened the refrigerator door. She felt coolness in front, heat in back as Sam moved in even closer behind her, brushing up against her rear, branding her through the thin fabric of her shorts.

He pressed even tighter, draping himself along her back and reaching over her shoulder. She could have stepped out of his way; she preferred not to, though she risked dropping the berry bowl when he nibbled briefly at her earlobe.

"You want to eat these or wear them?" she asked, barely able to breathe.

The idea appealed to him instantly. "Don't forget the whipped cream." He shook the can, allowing her barely enough room to turn around and close the refrigerator, remaining within a foot of her.

Cassie felt his penetrating gaze as he continued to shake the can; when she looked up she saw a devilish gleam in his eyes. "What?" she asked suspiciously.

He grinned, then relieved her of the bowl of berries and set it on the counter without even watching to make sure it landed safely. "Just trying to picture you in whipped cream."

She stepped backward, a disbelieving laugh escaping as she went. "Oh, no. Sa-am," she warned, holding up a small, delicate hand to ward him off.

He tossed the cap over his shoulder with a devil-may-care attitude.

She continued to back away. There were two doors leading off the kitchen. She found herself at the one to his bedroom. "Sam, I'm warning you." She realized the words didn't make much of a threat through her smile. "It'll taste better on the dessert."

He squirted a blob on his finger, then licked it off, slowly, watching her as she watched his tongue move lightly over his skin. "Only one way to find out for sure."

Cassie could barely swallow, wondering if he knew how erotic the movement was, how hot it made her. She turned to escape into his bedroom, to torment him as much as he tormented her, only to find Sam was even more fleet of foot than she remembered. She found herself lying facedown on his bed, his arms wrapped around her possessively, his body pressing her securely into the mattress.

He flipped her over effortlessly. She stared up into Sam's grinning face. He held up the can.

"No!" she squealed. All the squirming in the world wouldn't dislodge Sam as he straddled her, his thighs hugging her ribs, his hips pressing into her abdomen, though her squirming didn't amount to much more than a token against his strength.

Whipped cream landed on her neck, then trailed down toward her cleavage.

She could barely form words through her laughter. "I can't believe you're doing this to me."

Sam licked it all off and took his time doing it, pausing after each upward journey of his tongue to gauge her reaction. When every trace of it was gone, when her laughter stopped and her heartbeat soared, he followed with a squirt on each cheek. He sucked them off, one by one. Distracted, he let go of the can when Cassie reached for it.

She didn't bother to shake it again, just aimed directly for his chest.

"Now look what you've done." His eyes twinkled as he sat up straight, holding most of his weight off her. "I guess I'll just have to strip it off."

No sooner had he tugged off his T-shirt than Cassie let fly with more whipped cream. "My turn," she said, rising until they were chest to chest. "Lean back."

Sam watched her tongue dart out, flick across his skin, sending searing heat to lower regions. His eyes closed as she teased one nipple. "Cassie," he gasped.

"Hmm?" She gave the can a tiny shake, determined to thrill him as much as he had delighted her, only to feel Sam wrench it out of her hand. She heard it land on the floor somewhere. "Had enough?"

"No." He pushed her back down on the mattress, covered her with his half-naked body. "Never enough. Not with you."

As he captured and held her lips with his, his fingers found their way up the leg of her shorts and slipped under the elastic of her underwear. They crept higher, deeper, as her heart raced against his chest.

"Like this?" He touched her intimately, gently, and felt her shudder.

She barely nodded. Her only answer was to push herself against him.

He slipped her tank top over her head. "Thank you, thank you, thank you."

"What?" she asked in confusion.

"I didn't know how I was going to get a sports bra off you." He reached behind her.

"In front."

He unclasped her lacy bra and sent it flying, then covered her completely with hands that were never still, that engulfed her, sensitized her with the roughness they'd earned from hard, honest labor. She tried to unbutton his shorts, but couldn't get coordinated enough as he teased her nipples with his thumbs. He did it for her, then let her push his clothes down as far as she could reach, before she finished undressing him with her foot.

She took him in her hand, and he just barely remembered what he had to do.

"What's your favorite color?" he asked.

"The first one you reach."

He chuckled low in his throat and stroked her with his thumb. "We were made for each other."

# Chapter Thirteen

Cassie woke up in the morning, sunlight streaming through the bedroom window, with a very still bird lying stiff on its back next to her in the bed. Apparently the clasp on the screen door hadn't kept the hybrid macaw out, after all.

"George?" she whispered. "George?"

Nothing moved, not a feather, not an eyelid.

"Oh, my God, I rolled over and killed his bird."

Sam was nowhere to be seen or heard. Cassie reached out slowly and touched a long, red tail feather. "Oh, George—"

Instantly the inert form turned into a strutting, screaming mass of red indignation.

"My God!" Cassie yelled as she jumped to a sitting position and clapped her hands over her ears. The bird outyelled her by several decibels.

"What the hell—" Sam stormed into the room to find Cassie sitting naked in his bed, tangled in the sheets, a wary eye on the furious parrot. "George! How did you get in here?"

Feathers ruffled, beak open, George gave Cassie one long, threatening, irate glare. Careful not to make any sudden moves, Cassie inched a hand over, grabbed a pillow and held it up in front of her in self-defense. As Sam approached the bed, George ducked by him and raced out the door.

"What are you laughing at?" Cassie demanded as she hugged the pillow to her chest. "I was afraid he was going to bite off something vital."

"I've seen you threaten snakes, purposely try to attract a gator, kick men bigger than you—"

"All right, all right. I remember all of it."

"Bob's due soon."

She vaulted out of bed and headed for the bathroom. "I'll be out in a jiff."

Cassie finished quickly in the shower, rinsing off in record time.

Sam lounged in the bathroom doorway and watched her tug on her skins and sports bra.

Cassie scowled. "Must you stand there like that? There's nothing sexy about getting dressed in running clothes."

"Wanna bet?" He'd watch her slip into anything, as long as he could get her back out of it later. "I came in to tell you breakfast is ready."

"Wow, first dinner, now breakfast. What's left?"

"You'll see." Sam gave her a playful pat on her derriere as she strolled past him.

At the table, over pancakes and fruit, Cassie studied all the photos around her. "When you get in touch with the people about the road race, they'll want to know what kind of picture you want on the T-shirt."

He followed her gaze. "You mean I get to choose?"

"Sure. I figure you'll want a picture of a panther."

"Of course" he was quick to agree.

"Well, if you don't have some input, the picture might end up looking like a tiger or a black leopard."

He groaned. "I don't suppose they could copy a photo?"

"I don't know what they can do for the price. Just give them whatever they need so the picture comes out looking like one of a panther."

"But panthers all look different."

"Only to you, Sam."

"But look—" He got up and pointed at a picture on the wall. "Look at the expression in those eyes. And here—" He pointed to another. "They're totally different."

She sighed. "Like I said..."

"You really can't tell the difference?"

"Maybe after I'm around them some more. Maybe you could jot down some ideas for the flyers we'll circulate. You know, some statistics. But be brief. This is supposed to be a fun run."

"DO YOU HAPPEN to have a T-shirt to go over that outfit?"

Cassie was sitting on Sam's battered couch, bent over to tie her running shoes. "You're afraid I'll blind the panther with these colors?"

"He'll be fine. The press is here."

"The press?" she asked in surprise. "Here?"

"Yeah, it knocked the wind out of my sails, too. I'd hoped for a private little transfer here. I'm going out to talk to them. Meet you over by the pens."

Ordinarily Sam loved the press. His panthers—Florida's panthers—needed all the publicity they could get to save them.

Today, however, he was less than grateful. They could have waited a couple more weeks until the panther was released into the wild to do their publicity thing. Then the male could run off into the trees and be rid of all of them. Now he would not only be transferred from a cage to a pen, but he would be surrounded by a species he didn't understand and with whom he couldn't communicate.

"Are you releasing the panther on your property?" a businesslike reporter asked as Sam walked across the yard to where the press congregated in the driveway.

"Isn't that Cassie Osbourne's van?" another wanted to know, pointing over his shoulder.

The 4GOLDS plate was a dead giveaway.

"Have you convinced her not to build in the Everglades yet?"

"Has she changed her mind—"

"If you'll all please stay back here by the cars until we make the transfer, I'd appreciate it," Sam said. His tone indicated it was not a casual request. He stared down the first reporter who dared step forward. "Thank you."

Across the yard, Cassie slipped quietly off the porch and headed for the pens.

"Hey, how come she doesn't have to stay back?"

Sam followed the man's gaze, then stared him down, too. "When you save a panther's life on the highway, then I'll let you get closer. In the meantime, this is a panther who was never around people until he was hit. He's shy and he's frightened. You can all have a closer look—one at a time—as soon as he's safely in his new pen."

"Why is he here?"

"Will he be returned to the wild?"

"He's here temporarily. He needs antibiotics and observation." Sam could see that Bob was ready and waiting. "Excuse me. Please stay here until I let you know otherwise."

Cassie watched as the two men lifted the cage and panther down off the truck bed. She stepped forward once to help, but the two of them accomplished their task quickly and smoothly, butting the crate up against a small, open door in the pen.

Sam tried to reassure the animal with soft panther noises. Bob spoke softly. The reporters inched their way across the yard until they were within ten feet.

The panther remained in his cage.

"When is he coming out?"

"Panthers are very cautious," Sam explained. "He has to check things out first. When we release him back into the forest, you'll see him shoot out of his cage faster than a comet."

As soon as he decided the new pen seemed better than his crate, the panther headed straight for the den, inspected it, then disappeared inside.

"Okay, you can get a little closer. Please try not to get too loud. Don't rattle the fence. I'm sure you understand," Sam said with a smile meant to win them over. He could be pleasant when he needed to be, but one more step over the line and he'd have reporters for dinner—as the main course.

The half-dozen reporters zeroed in on Cassie.

"Miss Osbourne—"

"Cassie—"

"Have you canceled your plans—"

Sam threw up his hands and walked away. One of the last surviving Florida panthers was right in front of them, and who were they interested in? Cassie. He hoped she would do as well with their publicity this time as she had when he'd kept her under duress.

Sam turned and called back to her, loud enough to steer the conversation the right way, "Be sure to mention the race for the panthers."

Right on cue, the next question was "What race?"

Bob sat beside him on the porch steps and watched. "Can you believe it? A wild panther, and they'd rather talk to her. Makes you wonder if we're narrow-minded, doesn't it?"

"Us? Never. Now what?" Sam growled as several cars and pickup trucks pulled into his drive and parked. "It better not be any of those demonstrators I've seen on the news. They give everybody a bad name."

The dozen or so men and women paused, looked from Sam and Bob on the porch to the reporters and Cassie by the pens and chose to approach the latter.

"It makes you wonder what we're lacking," Sam said to his friend.

"Yeah, well, she's prettier than both of us put together." Bob suddenly noticed Sam staring hard at him. "Not that I noticed, of course...."

"I don't think it's Cassie they're interested in. We'd better go see what's up."

"Oh, I know what's up," Bob said as they rose. "That heavy guy there, up in front—he's mayor of Natchoon."

"Mayor? Why the heck—"

Bob shrugged as they quickly walked side by side toward the activity. "He probably wants to have his say to the media without the demonstrators getting equal time."

"If he knew they'd be here, chances are the rest of them will show up, too. Do me a favor, Bob."

"Sure. Anything."

"Grab a rifle and stand at the end of the driveway—"

Bob held up both hands. "Anything but that, buddy."

It was Sam's turn to shrug. "Well, I was just trying to keep it peaceful around here. No telling what that new male will do to hurt himself if we get a lot of commotion...."

"All right, all right. Jeez, does your mother know you're good with the guilt trips?"

"Take Bill along. Between the two of you, maybe we won't have to deal with the riffraff."

Sam turned away from Bob to hear the mayor talking.

"Natchoon has twenty unemployed men and women for every endangered panther," he told the reporters. "We're talking heads of households. Then there are spouses, kids...."

Sam tuned him out as he watched Cassie's face. It was plain to see she couldn't tune him out.

"There *will* be a factory, Uncle Ed," she interrupted.

*Uncle* Ed?

"When, girl? Every week we lose another family to Miami or Orlando. They're no better off there. You know that. At least in Natchoon they're with family, people who care."

"I just need a couple more weeks—"

"For what? We got the property, we got the men—"

"I'm still hoping for a different location."

Ed turned and looked over his shoulder, right into Sam's hard eyes. "For him, no doubt."

"Uncle Ed—"

He returned his full attention to her. "Need I remind you that when you needed us, we were there? When your dream was to go to the Olympics and you needed support, we were there—not once, but twice."

Cassie wanted to put her hands over her ears and block it all out. He was right, of course. She owed the entire town of Natchoon. That was how the whole project had gotten started. She had dreamed of producing her own line of running shoes someday; they had the recession and needed work soon—voilà! The idea was born over Sunday dinner, grew throughout the evening, blossomed at an emergency town meeting and was nurtured by her grandfather until he died.

When Cassie looked up at Sam, unable to hold eye contact, he knew he was as helpless as a drowning man in the ocean.

"Cassie..." He had only asked for a couple of weeks.

She held eye contact then but it was only bleak acceptance he saw. "Sam, I'm sorry," she whispered under the mayor's drone to the press.

Sam crossed his arms over his chest. "Two weeks."

Cassie glanced at the mayor and shook her head.

"I can't let you do this," Sam warned.

"I don't have any choice."

"Well, I do. Time to go," he announced to everyone. "The panthers are getting restless with this many people around."

There wasn't a panther to be seen, but no one argued as they took in Sam's defensive posture and cold glare.

Cassie hung back as the others drove away. "Sam..." Was this it? The end? Dismissal?

"I'd say I got rid of them none too soon," Sam commented as the reporters and townspeople met more cars at the road.

"That's not fair, Sam. They need—"

"*They* need?" he exploded. "What about what *I* need? What the panthers need? What about what you need, Cassie?" he concluded on a softer note.

She got into her car and closed the door. "I guess I need a man who understands."

Cassie could barely navigate through her tears and around all the cars and trucks and people yelling at one another. With her fingertips, she brushed away the wetness, only to have it renewed in duplicate.

"Cassie—"

She rolled up her window, not in the mood to talk to anyone or fight with anyone. She wanted to be alone for a good, long time, to pick up the pieces of her life.

Alone. That's what she would be now, and for a long, long time.

SAM HUNCHED in the glider on his porch.

How his life had changed since he'd met Cassie. For the first time he'd been focused on something other than panthers. For the first time someone else's dream had seemed almost as important as his.

He had a lot of phone calls to make. Finding Cassie another piece of land had turned out to be a pipe dream.

He had to get ready to fight for what he believed in.

CASSIE WAS AT the construction site at the break of dawn five days later, pacing back and forth, keeping an eye on every development. The foreman calmly worked his way through a thermos of coffee. Members of the crew trickled in, sometimes alone, sometimes two and three to a vehicle. Each checked in with the foreman. Work didn't begin until seven, and no one started early.

"You keep looking for someone," the foreman commented during a rare moment when he was alone with her.

Cassie dragged her eyes away from the dusty road. "Do I? I don't mean to."

"You expecting trouble?"

That was putting it mildly. "I hope not."

"Lady, we all hope not. But it's pretty hard to call all these guys up and tell them where to report to work and expect no one else to know."

She groaned inwardly, her hopes dashed that the demonstrators might not know. She might have had some sympathy for them as people if they had been demonstrating for something worthwhile—like preservation of the panthers. They barely mentioned the panthers in all their rantings and ravings to the press, however. They seemed more concerned about two tiny acres of trees.

The foreman stood up straighter and looked over Cassie's shoulder. "Maybe we'd better call for reinforcements."

Cassie turned and saw what he saw—a line of cars and trucks rapidly approaching, a wake of dust obscuring those in the rear. Too late.

The first wave of the invasion wasn't so bad. Finally, peaceful demonstrators. This group was head and shoulders above the radicals. These people knew how to conduct an organized sit-in.

She'd have to have them removed, of course. "Call the sheriff," she instructed the foreman. "You've heard the expression—time is money."

"Yes, ma'am."

The second wave was on her side. Uncle Ed and fifty others, men and women from Natchoon, most of them one relation or another to Cassie, were unhappy with the demonstrators sitting around on the ground, hugging trees. Outnumbering them two to one, they tried dragging them away, but the demonstrators kept going back. The townspeople showed them pictures of their children in tattered clothes, looking very hungry, trying to get the demonstrators to change their minds out of pure sympathy. Nothing worked, but they kept trying, always maintaining the peace.

Sam arrived next, and he slammed his truck door hard enough to shake the whole vehicle. He covered the ground in long, angry strides until he stood in front of Cassie, his arms crossed tightly over his chest, a scowl etched on his face, fire in his eyes. Reporters and photographers were on his heels, their cameras and tape recorders going.

He stopped three feet away and looked very formidable. "Anything you want to tell me?" he demanded with a growl.

Cassie closed the distance between them, not about to be intimidated by his size or his barely checked temper. "What about you?" she snapped. "I guess these are all your friends sitting around hugging my trees."

"Just doing what we can."

"Get off my land before I have you thrown in jail."

Without another word, he walked away and placed himself in front of a vibrating bulldozer.

Cassie glanced at her watch. "It's past time to start," she told the foreman.

He looked at her and shook his head. "Lady, I don't care if this is your land—"

She stomped over to the driver of the bulldozer and yelled up to him. "You're getting paid to knock down trees. Get to it."

He pointed at Sam and shouted down to her. "He's in my way."

She motioned him forward with her hands, a determined look on her face.

He hesitated, his hands on the controls.

Cassie put one foot on the bulldozer, ready to climb aboard, muttering beneath the rumble of the machine. "They're not just holding up earth-moving equipment here. They're stomping on my dream—my whole family's dream. Why can't they leave us alone to build the factory? Why can't they let us make shoes and provide jobs for everyone?"

She grabbed a handhold and boosted herself up.

The operator shut down the machine. "You move him, then I go forward." He squinted at Sam. "But I don't think he's moving."

Outraged, Cassie jumped down, stomped over to Sam and pushed him as hard as she could with both hands flat against his chest. It was like pushing a firmly rooted oak tree. He didn't even have to take a half step backward to maintain his balance.

Their attention was drawn back to the road as several speeding cars arrived, their blaring horns shattering the silence. The next wave. Men and women dressed in bloodred shirts jumped out of their vehicles, and they'd come prepared. Within seconds, they had chained themselves to every piece of earth-moving construction equipment.

Cassie groaned in frustration and kicked at a root in her path. "I don't believe it." This had to be the final wave of the invasion. No one else was left.

She saw her dream fade before her eyes. With attention like this, there would be no factory, no shoes, no jobs. Her financial backers would withdraw their funds, their promises if they thought she couldn't deliver. And with the media here in full force, they were sure to know by noon.

Sam took a step closer to her. "Cassie, please."

"Don't talk to me!" she screamed at him, trying not to let any tears of frustration escape to embarrass her. She was unsure where to go, what to do next. "Don't ever talk to me again."

"Please. Let's try to work this out."

"There's nothing to work out." She was unsuccessful. A tear slid down her cheek. "We need this. My whole family's counting on this to pull them back up. I can help them if everyone would just leave us alone."

"Maybe—"

"Maybe you ought to go." She turned her back on him. She couldn't let him see her cry. She couldn't let everyone see her cry.

"I can't."

A reporter dared approach beneath Sam's glare. "Miss Osbourne—"

Before he had time to ask his question, Cassie grabbed the camera from the woman beside him. Without hesitation, she jerked it open and ripped out the film. One movement of her arms, and it was exposed and lying on the ground, damaged beyond repair, much as her life was.

"What will you do now?" the reporter asked, guarding his microphone carefully.

"The sheriff's on his way. I have a legal right to build here. Everyone who doesn't leave immediately will be arrested."

She felt Sam close behind her. "Cassie..."

"Including this man," she added. "I'm sure he'll be charged with inciting a riot."

"Now—"

She turned on him. "Well, what would you call it? Your friends have chained themselves to the equipment."

His eyes answered her. His friends were the peaceful ones, not the ones with chains who were chanting "My life for a tree. A tree for my life."

"Never mind. I'll wait for the sheriff." He resumed his place in front of the bulldozer.

"Have you called the sheriff yet?" Cassie demanded of the foreman.

"Too late. He was already on his way."

"Already . . ." Cassie studied Sam, wondering what he had been up to.


"I GOT a restraining order," the sheriff stated upon his arrival.

Cassie watched everyone leave, every last person, until she stood there alone. The equipment remained, a statement of hope that they would all be back soon.

She brushed away a tear and looked up at the sky. Her arms were folded across her chest, trying to hold everything in. All her sorrow. All her pain. All her dreams.

"You know what's really strange?" She spoke to the only person worth talking to right now—herself. "I understand why he did it. He's taken all my dreams and crushed them, and I still understand. I hurt enough to die, but I still respect him."

He should know he was so lucky.

"I thought I'd want to kill him. I ought to want to. I at least deserve to feel that."

Slowly, with an uncustomary drag in her step, she walked over to her van and opened the door. Visions of Sam filled the cab, memories of when he'd ridden with her. She forced them from her mind.

"I said I understood. That doesn't mean I can forgive him."

# Chapter Fourteen

"Cassie, telephone. It's another one."

*Not another one.*

Cassie sat with her head down on the desk. Since the news had broken the day before, all her investors had gotten nervous. If she couldn't deliver, they were going to put their money somewhere else. They weren't earning enough leaving it in the bank, waiting for her to straighten things out.

She absentmindedly wiped her fingers across her cheek, dabbing at the moisture that seemed to be there perpetually.

"Heard you got a little problem down there." It was her investor from Chicago.

"Just a minor setback," she said with all the confidence she could muster. "I'm sure we'll be back on track within days."

"Interest rates are too low for that money to just sit there in the bank, you know. I need a return on my money, Cassie. If you can't handle it..." He left the sentence unfinished.

"I can handle it. Trust me."

SAM CONSULTED with the track club, got the design right with the T-shirt people, then started to worry. He knew nothing about racing.

In short, he couldn't do it without Cassie. As much as he knew she'd probably try to maim him the instant she could get her hands on him, he had to follow through. He needed the money for the panthers, to house them, feed them, keep them healthy and fit.

He needed Cassie for himself.

"Somebody to see you," Cassie's secretary announced, then left Cassie and him alone.

He stood in the doorway and assessed her mood, reluctant to enter without an invitation. She sat at her desk, legs stretched out, feet up. Body language indicated she wasn't going to kill him instantly, but, then, she'd looked pretty calm when she'd kicked that poacher halfway into his next life.

She raised her head from where it had been resting on the back of the chair. She said nothing.

He held the T-shirt by the shoulders and let it drape downward, then raised it until it lay against his chest. "I chose emerald green. To match your eyes."

She looked away, out the window, as her vision blurred.

His heart broke again. "Do you like it?"

She nodded. "It'll go over well. It's a nice change from all the pastels."

"They need you."

She looked back at him.

"The panthers," he explained. "Achilles. They need you to put on this race. To buy them food, medicine, bigger pens. Only you can do that."

She shrugged.

"I need you."

She snorted. "Give me a break. You don't need anybody."

He hadn't thought she'd buy that, knowing her. Oh, he did need her. He was finding it hard to live without her, but he didn't think she'd believe him anytime this century.

He could tell her he loved her, but she'd think he was just trying to get his way. He had to show her. A picture was worth a thousand words, they said.

His hand passed restlessly over the T-shirt still draped on his chest, near the region of his heart. "The shirt people suggested we go with a different color every year. I know how you like bright colors. Maybe hot pink next year? Royal purple the next? Lemon yellow?"

"Whatever."

"Your autograph looks good across the back. It's a good endorsement for the cause. I'm kind of surprised you did it."

She sighed and stood up. "I've always liked your panthers, Sam. I have nothing against them. You know that. There's room for both of us."

"Come to the race with me then."

"I can't."

"Yes, you can. There's nothing you can't do. You're Cassie Osbourne."

She strolled over to the window and stared down at the street below. "I can't work with you, Sam."

"Why not?"

"It hurts too much."

He hadn't thought she'd admit to that—ever. It was reassuring. "Just until the race is over. Everything's in the works, Cassie. People expect you to be there. We can't just let it die now."

Her hand moved near her eyes. He was sure it wiped away a tear.

"Please."

She nodded then, and he felt great relief. Everything started with that first step, then another and another. The door was open, so to speak. He had his foot in.

The voice of Cassie's secretary filtered in from the outer office. "Telephone."

Cassie turned away from the window and back toward the desk. Sam caught her eye, but she said nothing to him.

"It's Chicago again. He's starting to sound nervous," her secretary added.

Sam watched as Cassie took a deep breath and turned her back on him.

"Cassie Osbourne," she said into the receiver.

She sounded so positive, almost normal. Sam knew better as she wiped away another tear with the back of her hand.

"Just allergies," she said into the phone. "Nothing to slow me down."

He turned and left then, but not before hearing her tell the caller that everything was going fine, that her lawyers would have it all worked out within hours.

RACE DAY DAWNED clear and crisp. If Cassie couldn't sleep the night before she raced, it was nothing compared with the night before holding a race.

She'd listened to weather reports for days.

"I don't know why I'm doing this," she told herself. "They're never right."

She listened, anyway.

They were right this time.

Cassie wore the emerald green panther shirt that proclaimed RUN FOR THE PANTHERS below Achille's picture. She dressed in short skins out of habit, even though she wasn't racing today. A French braid took her no time at all.

She arrived at the race site before everyone except Sam, and parked behind him. He unbuckled one of his brand new seat belts and strolled back to the van on the curb side.

He wore extremely faded, snug jeans beneath his panther T-shirt. Cassie noted that he looked dynamite in emerald green, but said nothing.

He smiled through the passenger window. "Great morning, isn't it?" He paused, but got no reply. "I thought you'd be early," he continued agreeably. "I got here early so I could help you with any last-minute stuff."

She still said nothing.

"Bad mood, huh?" He opened the passenger door.

Cassie bolted out the other side. There was no way she could sit there in the confines of the van with him.

"Yum, strawberries," he crooned as he reached into the open cooler between the seats and helped himself. "Got any whipped cream?"

Cassie looked back against her will—a mistake, she told herself as he popped the fruit into his mouth and grinned.

She walked away, barely able to make her legs work.

He followed. "So. What's next?" he asked as though no hot thoughts were replaying through either of their minds.

"The track club handles it from here" was all she said—was all she *could* say at that point. She needed a cup of water, and not to drink.

"Oh. Do they have all the equipment? The timer? The cones? The numbers?"

She nodded.

"Aren't you going to fire the starting gun?"

She turned on him, ready to snap his head off for his incessant questions.

He had the gall to smile at her.

"What is your problem?" she demanded.

"Me? I don't have a problem. No, ma'am. Not me."

"Well, I'm glad one of us doesn't," she snapped. "And no, I'm not firing the gun. Unless it's at you."

If her cool manner didn't get rid of him, she'd run. If he followed her, she'd run hard enough that he wouldn't be able to talk. She jogged away.

He not only followed her, he jogged beside her.

"Rough week?" he asked.

She jogged faster. Unfortunately she did have to stop in a half mile and stretch, but she'd keep her back to him.

He stretched alongside her, watching her carefully and doing exactly as she did, but said nothing more.

She followed the ten-kilometer course and checked it out for whatever hazards might have shown up between the time it had been mapped out and this morning. Five miles later, he was still with her. Fortunately he kept to himself. She was free to think about whatever she wanted.

He seemed different this morning; different from the only time she'd seen or spoken to him since she'd told the bulldozer operator to run him over. He seemed . . . almost back to his normal, good-natured self. As though he'd worked something out but wasn't telling her.

Well, if he thought their differences were just going to go away, he was sadly mistaken.

The calendar had worked against her. She knew now there was no way she could find a compromise, no way she could have both Sam and her factory. The lawyers were pushing ahead with the permits. The restraining order was going to fall, and she would go ahead and break ground.

She slowed her pace, sorely conscious of the tower of strength running along beside her. Could she live without him?

She didn't think so.

Would it really take too long to get new financing to build somewhere else? Perhaps not.

Couldn't the unemployed people get jobs somewhere else in the meantime? They hadn't been able to so far.

"Sam?"

"Yeah?"

She looked up at him, still jogging beside her. "I'm going to tell you something, but I don't want you to think it changes anything."

"What's that?"

"I love you."

Whether she sped up or he just stopped in shock was unclear, but either way, she continued on alone. Tears blurred her vision, but she knew he wasn't beside her anymore.

"Well, I'll be damned," Sam murmured as he slowed to a walk. "She said it."

He walked the short distance back to the vehicles alone, thinking, planning. Hoping.

The race kept them busy. Even though the track club was officially in charge, there was plenty to do and not enough bodies to do it. Sam helped out where he could, managed to stay right by Cassie's side, sometimes underfoot.

"Sam, cut it out."

"What?"

"That's the fourth time you've run into me."

"Sorry." His smile was not contrite. "Just trying to stay out of the runners' way."

"Well . . ." She turned back to business.

"I love you, too, you know," he said quietly.

She fumbled and almost dropped the ring of numbers she was holding.

There, he'd said it. When he was done with her, she wouldn't be able to claim he said it only to get her to change her mind. He had an alternate plan.

"Doesn't change anything, though," he added, much as she had. "If you fire up those bulldozers, I'll be right there in front of them again."

"No ifs about it. That factory's going up soon. A lot of people are counting on me."

"Yeah," he said with an exaggerated sigh. "I know how it is to have someone counting on you."

She glared at him.

"Of course, if I were to tell you that I'd found an empty factory where you could start production even sooner..." He let the thought linger, gave her time to absorb it without cramming it down her throat.

"You know I can't afford to buy a factory. All the financing I've been able to get is for building on land I own, then starting production. If I have to buy both a building *and* land, then I can't afford to buy equipment and hire people."

He'd gone over the details carefully on the phone the night before. There was no way she could lose on this deal. "Well, what if you were to put up future sales profits in lieu of financing until the purchase price is paid off?"

"Dream on. It'll be ages before I show a profit. There's start-up, marketing, personnel, overhead...." She answered a call for assistance at the chutes, jogging away from him without a backward glance.

Not one to give up easily, Sam followed her. "Sometimes all it takes is knowing the right people."

"Where have I heard that before? Sam, no one is going to make those arrangements with me. Everyone wants to see something for their money."

"Someone might do it for me...and for the panthers."

She stared at him and almost missed doing her job directing the first runners to their respective chutes. It was an easy job, something a child could do. "You're distracting me," she complained.

"I love distracting you."

"Get lost."

"I've found a building."

She continued her job. Runners farther back, and a little out of their league, were too exhausted to listen attentively when directed to their chutes.

Sam spent a few minutes helping out, not in any particular hurry to lay all his cards on the table. They'd dealt with this problem for weeks before he'd found a solution. Ten or fifteen minutes more wouldn't make or break them.

"I've found owners who are willing to finance the factory with a stock arrangement, too," he said when there was a lull after the finish of the race.

"You mean I should give away control before I even get started?" she snapped.

He smiled down at her. "I love it when you ball up your fists on your hips like that."

"It means I'm mad," she said through clenched teeth.

He laughed and rubbed his hand over his smooth-shaven jaw. "I know what it means. And you wouldn't have to give up any control. I know it's your company, your dream. You'd still be in complete charge."

She frowned at him, hands still on her hips. His only clue that she wasn't ready to jump down his throat was that the fists had relaxed.

"Is this all on the up-and-up? Or are you just trying to get me to delay breaking ground while your environmental lawyers try some new trick?"

"I'd never trick you, Cassie. I love you."

She mulled it over. "I know hundreds of people counting on employment in my factory. Where's your building located?"

"About thirty miles from Natchoon. It sits on ten acres, and it's been vacant for over a year. And it's not *my* building—it's yours, if you want it. With carpooling, it could work out well.''

She tilted her head and looked at him from a different perspective. ''Is this legit, Sam? Because if it's not—''

''It is. I swear. I've been making calls for—it seems like forever. I've made a lot of contacts over the years,'' he explained.

''It sounds too good to be true.''

''I know.''

''I've been turning it over in my mind constantly—it seems like twenty-four hours a day. I couldn't come up with anything.''

''I know. Me, too, for a while. Then I thought, hey, why not make some calls, run it by some people? Couldn't hurt. Might help.'' He shrugged as though it were nothing. In fact, he didn't want a lot of credit for this. He just wanted the path ahead to be a little clearer for them.

''I'll let you know.'' She turned and walked away.

Cassie walked around, alone, while the second race took place. As a businesswoman, she couldn't just hear about someone giving her carte blanche on an empty building—from a third party, no less—and assume everything would work out satisfactorily.

Had Sam explained what business she was in? He had no idea of her projections for the future, how long before she expected to see a profit, how much or how little that profit would be.

Sam had obviously put forth a great deal of effort to find her an alternate site for manufacturing her running shoes. Not just any shoes. She planned on changing the future of the sport with her innovative designs. She, as a world record holder and Olympic champion, *knew* what was needed in a shoe.

An empty building, he'd said. She could begin production sooner, hire people sooner, get her product on the market sooner.

Her relatives could get to work that much sooner, save their homes, stay together.

She might lose her tax incentives if she didn't build on the designated property. Then again, she might not.

She wouldn't lose Sam.

It was then that she realized what she'd almost given up. For tax incentives, for a small head start, she'd almost given up the love of her life? The mere thought of such stupidity astounded her. If she did it right, she wouldn't have to give up anything important. Surely she could compromise on a lot of little issues so she could have both big ones.

Cassie stood up tall and straight and took a deep breath. "I almost let a great guy get away. And for what? A business?"

She felt her forehead to see if she were feverish. "Nah, just coming to my senses. Finally."

She made herself slow down, put her excitement on a back burner long enough to think things through thoroughly. She had no specifics on this building Sam said he had found. She didn't know what size it was. She didn't know how it was constructed or how it was laid out. She didn't know anything about the owners or what they were willing to do to finance it—which for her meant they would have to do absolutely everything for the first couple of years.

"So," Cassie assured herself with a sigh, "it doesn't

matter. It just doesn't matter. If this building isn't already perfect, I'll make do. If some guy I don't even know is willing to help me out, then I'm willing to make concessions, too.''

She strolled along, oblivious to people watching her talk to herself as if someone were right beside her.

''Cassie! Time for the awards,'' the secretary of the track club called out to her.

The awards table was set up on wide, concrete steps, with all the trophies and plaques on display. The crowd relaxed on the grassy circle in front of the steps. It was a social group of several thousand; some were sitting, some standing, all were in small groups passing the time of day. They snacked on hot dogs and pretzels, soda and beer.

From his truck, Sam retrieved several things. First he grabbed the rolled-up factory blueprints, plot plan and topographical maps, then a small, plain box that fit easily in the palm of his hand.

When Cassie arrived at the awards area, he waved her over with the roll of diagrams. ''I thought you might like to see these.'' He rolled them out on an empty corner of the table. ''It's the building I was telling you about.''

She barely glanced at them.

''Come on,'' he coaxed. He hadn't counted on her being so stubborn once he'd told her the good news. ''At least look it over.''

She shrugged while her eyes roamed up his muscular arm, then looked away. ''It doesn't matter.''

He rolled the diagrams back up with short, staccato twists of his hands. He pretended it was her neck. ''You won't even consider this building?''

She smiled up at him. "I wouldn't consider anything else."

He slapped the roll against the tabletop. "You—" He stopped abruptly. Had he heard her correctly? "What?" he asked skeptically, not sure whether to trust his own ears.

"If it's not perfect, I'm sure we can make it work. I do have one question about the lot, though."

He was afraid to say anything for fear she'd change her mind. He rolled the papers back out on the table; he held one side down while she held the other.

"It looks pretty flat around back here," she said pointing to the rear of the lot. "Do you think there's any chance I could put in a track for training?"

"We can ask. So? You'll take this?" He wanted everything to be perfectly clear.

She nodded. "You call your friend. I'll call my lawyers. When can I see the building?"

"I have the keys in my pocket."

She glanced at her watch. "How about after the awards?"

"How about I take you to lunch first to celebrate?"

"Deal." She stuck out her hand.

"OUR FIRST AWARD, for overall winner of the men's ten-kilometer..." the president of the track club announced over the microphone.

Sam handed the trophy to the winner, and both he and Cassie shook hands with him.

"This is a great thing you did for the panthers," Sam said quietly to her as she handed him the next trophy to pass out.

"It's nothing compared with what you do every day," she demurred. "You're the one they depend on twenty-four hours a day, day in and day out. You're the one with the dream."

"You think what I do is special?"

She handed him the next trophy, and didn't pull away when his fingers lingered gently on her hand. "Definitely. I'll be helping runners with my shoes, friends and relatives with jobs, but you help the underdog." She added with a grin, "So to speak."

"Yeah?"

"Sam, most people only dream. You carry yours out. You're the only one who can do what you do." She gave him a small shove toward the next winner waiting for his trophy.

"Would you like to help?"

She smiled. "Sure. Why not?"

"Do you think you'd like panther kittens running through the house?"

She laughed lightly at the picture that presented— little, fluffy, spotted kittens tumbling over one another, trying to climb the couch, playing hide-and-seek beneath it, pouncing on bare toes. "Who wouldn't?" Maybe she could visit often, pretend they were her kittens in her house.

"First woman runner overall for the ten-kilometer..." the president continued.

Sam handed Shelly her trophy and shook her hand. Cassie gave her a big hug.

"Friend of yours?" he asked quietly after Shelly had left the steps.

She shot him a big smile. "Future Olympic champion, too, as soon as I get her in a pair of my running shoes."

"Modest, aren't you?"

"Hey, you do your thing, I'll do mine."

He said nothing for a few minutes, and Cassie paused to wonder why.

"How about you help me do my thing?" he asked as he handed out one of the last trophies.

"Sure. Anytime."

"I mean all the time."

Their eyes met and locked. Neither Sam nor Cassie moved.

The president of the track club noisily cleared his throat. "Next trophy, guys," he said, hinting they keep their minds on business, not each other.

"Oh," Cassie said with a start. She read the inscription to be sure she had the right one, then shoved it at Sam to hand out. "Sorry," she said to the track-club members who stood around, making no attempt to hide their friendly amusement at her expense.

She looked up at Sam. He had a big smile on his face and *he* wasn't in the least embarrassed to have been caught with his mind not on his job. He grinned at the attentive crowd as though he had them in the palm of his hand. She thought about stepping on his foot.

"How about it?" he asked.

She didn't like not knowing the question. "How about what?"

"Helping me out—all the time."

The trophies were all passed out. Cassie looked around and saw that people weren't leaving, but were all waiting expectantly. "You'll have to be more specific."

He pointed to the table.

No wonder the crowd was still there. There was something left to give out, though she didn't know what it could be. She picked up the small box, shook it a little to be sure there was something in it, then held it out to Sam.

"Open it," he said.

Her mouth was agape as she took the lid off the tiny box. "It's your panther ring, Sam. Oh, you're not giving this away, are you?" She looked down at the crowd. Some lucky person was getting quite a door prize.

"Depends."

She looked up at him, then held out the box and ring again. If he wanted to give it away, it was his business. She knew it must mean a lot to him; she'd never seen him without it—not in the jungle, not in bed, not in the shower, not even when he was working in the pens. It was as much a part of him as the gravelly tone in his voice.

He took the ring but wouldn't release her hand. He took a deep breath. "Cassie Osbourne, will you marry me?"

"What?" Her mouth dropped open.

"I can't afford a honeymoon to a tropical island. I can't even afford to take the time off. But I will be the most devoted husband this world has ever seen if you'll have me."

She just stood there, astounded beyond words. *Devoted* wasn't in question here. Sam had proved beyond a doubt that he could devote himself to anything, full time.

"I also couldn't afford a new diamond engagement ring...."

She reached out and gently took the ring from his grasp. The tiny diamond eye sparkled. "I've never seen you without this on your finger."

"I never want to see you without it on yours. Come raise panthers with me. Marry me, Cassie." It wasn't a question, but a declaration.

She understood the difference. She handed him the ring back.

He paused, seemingly unsure what to do.

She held up her left hand. "Yes," she whispered, for his ears only. "I want you to put it on me."

To her surprise and delight, the crowd went wild with cheers as Sam slipped the gold ring on her finger. She'd never be without it, or him, again.

Once in a while, there's a man so special, a story so different, that your pulse races, your blood rushes. We call this

Gabriel Falconi is one such man, and FALLING ANGEL is one such book. Two years after his death, Gabriel is back on earth. He's still drop-dead handsome with his long black hair. But this time he's here to right three wrongs he'd done in his earthly life. Will this fallen angel earn his wings?

# FALLING ANGEL
## by

*Anne Stuart*

Don't miss the first of these sexy, special heroes. They'll make your HEARTBEAT!

Available in December wherever Harlequin books are sold. Watch for more Heartbeat stories, coming your way soon!

*1993 Keepsake*

*Stories*

Capture the spirit and romance of Christmas with KEEPSAKE CHRISTMAS STORIES, a collection of three stories by favorite historical authors. The perfect Christmas gift!

Don't miss these heartwarming stories, available in November wherever Harlequin books are sold:

ONCE UPON A CHRISTMAS by Curtiss Ann Matlock
A FAIRYTALE SEASON by Marianne Willman
TIDINGS OF JOY by Victoria Pade

# ADD A TOUCH OF ROMANCE TO YOUR HOLIDAY SEASON WITH KEEPSAKE CHRISTMAS STORIES!

HX93